'I don't have ti...
Samuel stated.

'So you've *never* had a relationship?' ... asked incredulously.

'Of course I have,' he admitted. 'I was even married for a while there, but it didn't work out.'

'Why?' she asked.

'It's none of your business,' he said, laughing at her obvious irritation. 'All right, I'll word it better. I'm not husband material.'

His pager interrupted her protests. 'Saved by the bell,' Samuel said. 'Now let's get back to it.'

As she followed him down the corridor her mind was whirring. Why would someone as gorgeous and sensual as Samuel Donovan vow himself off relationships?

Carol Marinelli did her nursing training in England and then worked for a number of years in casualty. A holiday romance while backpacking led to her marriage and emigration to Australia. Eight years and three children later the romance continues... Today she considers both England and Australia her home. The sudden death of her father prompted a reappraisal of her life's goals and inspired her to tackle romance writing seriously.

Recent titles by the same author:

DR CARLISLE'S CHILD
THE OUTBACK NURSE

THE EMERGENCY ASSIGNMENT

BY
CAROL MARINELLI

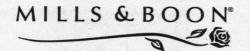

MILLS & BOON®

For Mum with love

First published in Great Britain 2001
Harlequin Mills & Boon Limited,
Eton House, 18-24 Paradise Road, Richmond, Surrey TW9 1SR

© Carol Marinelli 2001

ISBN 0 263 82720 8

Set in Times Roman 10½ on 12 pt.
03-0202-50706

Printed and bound in Spain
by Litografia Rosés, S.A., Barcelona

CHAPTER ONE

'GUESS who's got a meeting with the production team at eight-thirty on Monday?' Erin Casey burst in to the lounge room, dropping her bag as she entered and impatiently kicking off her shoes. 'And it's not going to be some ten-minute fill-in this time. I'm going to be given the prime-time slot.' She jumped on to the sofa beside her sister and sat cross-legged as Anna carefully replaced her bookmark and with a resigned smile placed her book on the coffee-table.

'Who told you?' Anna asked, her calm voice a sharp contrast to her elder sister's excited chatter.

'Dave did. He's going to be the chief cameraman for whatever it is they've got up their sleeves. And from the way they're talking, Dave is sure it's going to be something big, and they want *me* to do it. I just knew there was something in the air—my horoscope said this was going to be a month of once-in-a-lifetime opportunities. It must be something to do with the election.'

Anna laughed. 'And you've got tabs on interviewing the Prime Minister?'

'Well, who knows? Maybe they want a fresh approach.'

'They'd certainly get that with you, but just don't go getting your hopes up till you've found out first hand. You know how quickly things change there.'

Erin nodded. 'I know, but they can't expect me to keep on doing reports on the latest weight-loss scams or dodgy builders. This is going to be big, I can just *feel* it.

Anyway, we'll know more on Monday. What do you fancy for dinner, Anna? It's my turn to cook so I thought we might try out the new pizza place.'

'That's not cooking, Erin.' Anna smiled. 'But don't worry about me, I'm going out with Jordan tonight. You're not the only one with big news. I've got some of my own actually.' She held out her hand and was almost knocked off the sofa as Erin let out a squeal of delight and flung herself at Anna.

'You're engaged? When did it happen? Why didn't you tell me? Here's me rabbiting on about some silly television show while you're sitting there with this huge piece of news!' Erin sat back up and pulled Anna's hand to her face, her large emerald green eyes examining the tasteful diamond solitaire. 'It's beautiful,' she gasped. 'Absolutely beautiful. Can I try it on?'

Anna pulled the precious ring off her finger. 'It will be miles too big for you,' she warned as Erin slipped the ring on.

Closing her tiny fingers together to stop the ring from slipping, deliberately ignoring her bitten nails, Erin admired the stone.

'So when did Jordan ask you?'

'Today. He picked me up from the library at lunchtime, so I thought there was something going on. He'd organised a beautiful picnic lunch, and we went down by the Yarra River and he just asked me, right out of the blue. Apparently he'd asked Miss Heatherton if I could have the afternoon off days ago, so they were all in on it. I thought it was strange—just before lunchtime Miss Heatherton suddenly told me to go and tidy myself up a bit and put on some lipstick or something. She said I was looking frightfully pale.'

Anna's beaming face grew serious suddenly. 'He

didn't know what to do, whether he should ask your permission or something.'

'Ask me? Don't be silly.' Erin managed a laugh but a huge lump suddenly filled her throat.

'Well, you're the one who brought me up. I told him he'd only embarrass you. We're going over to tell his parents tonight and I thought next Saturday we might all go out to celebrate—nothing big, just the two families. I don't want a big fuss.'

'That would be lovely, but if you think you're getting away with a small wedding you can forget it. There's enough money for a proper wedding for you—I made sure of that when...well, you know.' Erin gave her sister a hug. 'Mum and Dad would have been so proud. You know that, don't you?'

Anna leant against her sister. 'I hope so. I'm sure they'd have liked Jordan.'

Erin squeezed her sister. 'What's not to like? He's good-looking, kind, he's got a great future as a lawyer and he makes you happy. Now, don't you dare start crying. Do you want to face your future in-laws with red, puffy eyes?'

But Erin's words didn't stop the tears that spilled out down Anna's cheeks. 'I know I haven't been easy, I know I gave you a hard time when I was a teenager. I just want you to know how much I appreciate everything...'

Erin cut her short. 'Save it for the wedding speeches. Now, come on, you'd better get ready—it's almost seventhirty and you know how punctual Jordan is.'

Anna rolled her eyes. 'Don't remind me. Living with Jordan is going to be very strange after so long with you. It's going to feel weird, sharing a house with someone who actually puts their clothes in the laundry and tidies up behind themselves.'

Erin grinned. 'You'll miss me really.' She kept up the light-hearted banter, kept the smile on her face as she helped Anna get ready, and, ever watchful of her little sister, checked she had her asthma pumps in her handbag.

'We don't want you wheezing over the lobster,' she joked. But by the time Jordan had been and she had kissed her future brother-in-law on the cheeks and opened a bottle of champagne and toasted their happiness, it was actually a relief when she waved them off and could finally stop smiling. Making her way back into the huge house, she picked up her champagne glass and walked over to the mantelpiece. Picking up a picture, she stared at the image. Mum and Dad standing so straight and smiling, their faces full of pride. Anna, eleven years old and awkward in front of the camera, her long raven curls, just like their mother's, framing her round pretty face, spoiled by an angry frown—a tell-tale sign of the difficult adolescent she would become.

And there she was: eighteen years old, as skinny and scrawny then as she was now, holding an excited puppy in her arms. Her mousy brown hair was worn in a short spiky style, much the same as now, except for the blonde foils that added a bit of lightness. She had always hated her hair but ages ago had realised it would never grow long like Anna's.

Erin touched her mother's smiling face. She could remember that day so vividly—she had just been accepted to study journalism at uni. Her father was holding the newspaper containing her exam results that meant she would get into Melbourne University. How happy that day had been. How could they have guessed as they'd stood in the garden of their affluent Camberwell home that just two days later all their dreams would be shattered? That Marcus and Grace Casey would be killed in a horrific motor vehicle accident, leaving their two beloved daughters orphans.

'She's happy, Mum and Dad, so don't worry.' Erin spoke to the picture as she did often. Carefully replacing the frame on the mantlepiece, she made her way into the kitchen and surveyed the contents of the fridge. It had been her turn to shop this week and, of course, she hadn't got around to it. All that was there was the suspicious-looking remains of a vegetable lasagne that looked well past its use-by date and a cold chicken salad Anna had prepared for her lunch tomorrow. A strict vegetarian, Erin gave a sigh.

'Oh, well, two-minute noodles again,' she said to Hartley, the fat golden Labrador who dozed in the corner.

Erin didn't mind her own company. In fact, she usually enjoyed nothing more than a night in by herself and the chance to burn some aromatic oils and practise her meditation or write to her child sponsors dotted around the globe, but tonight the house just seemed empty.

She was pleased for Anna—nothing was more important to Erin than her sister's happiness. But, though she hated herself for it, Erin couldn't help but feel just the tiniest bit jealous. Anna, at twenty-one, had it all worked out, while she herself seemed to be cruising somewhat aimlessly at the moment. As much as she raved about her career, it wasn't really going as well as she'd hoped. She'd accepted the job as a news reporter on a local current affairs show, thinking it would be her big break. Little had she known when she'd taken the job that the network would, within a week of her starting, slash the budget, forcing the resignations of most of the show's big names, along with the big stories.

The one consolation had been that the reduced budgets—and therefore reduced staff—had increased her status somewhat, so at least she got her name twice in the credits—once as reporter and once as co-producer. But it was hardly riveting stuff. Her time was mainly spent chasing used car salesmen and the like across yards as she 'exposed' their latest scams. And the only piece of her anatomy to appear on screen to date had been her derriere as she'd escaped over the nearest fence.

Despite her excited declarations to Anna about Monday being her big chance, Erin knew deep down that she would no more be interviewing the Prime Minister than flying to the moon. But it wasn't just work that was causing this melancholy: the fact Anna was getting married and leaving only seemed to amplify the lack of her own social life recently. Sure, she had lots of friends, but as the terrible thirties loomed ever nearer, most of her friends were by now in stable relationships and starting to have children, leaving Erin feeling somewhat deserted.

Not that she needed a man to make her feel good— Erin was far too liberated and independent to rely on a man for her happiness. But still, she mused, it would be nice to have someone special in her life and, grudgingly she admitted to herself, to have someone standing in the pews to quell the 'three times a bridesmaid' remarks when she inevitably did her duty as Anna's bridesmaid. 'Fat chance.' Erin said out loud.

There wasn't even the slightest hint of a romance coming in Erin's direction, not even the tiniest blip on the horizon. She looked slowly around at the living room. It wasn't a shrine as such but not much had changed since her parents had died. But things were going to change now and she acknowledged that. The house was already far too big for the two of them, let alone once Anna had gone. Erin felt a flutter of nervousness. Times were certainly changing.

'But it's been done before, lots of times,' Erin protested, then bit her tongue. The last thing she wanted was for them to give the job to someone else, but how could she tell her superiors the real reason for her anxiety? That Melbourne City Hospital held too many memories for her to do an objective report, that just the mention of the place sent Erin into a cold sweat. If her superiors realised that it was in the very same emergency department that Erin's own parents had died, they probably wouldn't have even considered her for the position.

'Then it's up to you to do it differently.' Mark Devlet, the director, cut sharply into her thoughts. 'There's a lot of public interest about the waiting times in Melbourne City A and E, along with the staff pressures. There's a hell of a lot of material there, though admittedly a Monday or Tuesday might have proved more politically newsworthy but the hospital board weren't having a bar of it. Jack said they were the days when the waiting times for patients to get up to the ward seemed to skyrocket. Still a Saturday night should turn up a few gems. It's up to you to make it interesting.

'And you're wrong, Erin, it hasn't been done at Melbourne City before. They've never allowed cameras in there until now, so it's a real scoop. Jack Duncan has been working on the hospital for ages, and if an early election hadn't been announced he'd be right on to it. We've got to strike while the iron's hot, before the board of directors at the hospital change their minds.'

Erin nodded. She'd seen the bad press the emergency department at Melbourne City had been generating recently. And as bitter as her memories were of the place, they were also tinged with a strange sense of loyalty. Agonising though her time there had been, the pain of the past was also peppered with glimmers of, if not fond memories exactly, a sense of peace. The tender compassion the staff had shown her, the dignified way they had treated her parents—all of this had helped her to get through the awful ensuing months.

Erin felt her throat tighten as she recalled one of the more poignant moments. A young staff nurse telling her she'd have to wait a while longer to see her parents as the doctor was still stitching her mother. And later, as she was led in to say goodbye, Erin recalled herself marvelling at the tender skill of the young doctor who had taken the time to make Grace Casey look presentable. The young doctor who had used the finest thread to suture her face even though Grace was already dead.

And as she recalled the painful memories, Erin knew that she must take the assignment—she had to do her best to show the real story behind the newspaper headlines.

Her composure restored, she flashed an assured smile at Mark. 'We could look at things from a different angle,' she said quickly, the excitement in her starting to mount. 'The viewers see enough blood and gore from all those fly-on-the-wall documentaries, so maybe we should—'

Mark Devlet cut her short. 'Don't rule out the blood and gore too much. The public do like it. But I agree it needs a different angle. Now, we've been given unlimited access, which is a miracle really. All the usual rules apply—the patients and relatives have to be informed about the filming and you have to clearly identify yourself.'

'I'll have a camera team beside me—I'm sure they'll get the drift that I'm a reporter.'

Mark grinned at her enthusiasm. 'The only fly in the

ointment is a Mr Samuel Donovan. He's the accident and emergency consultant and he's apparently very opposed to having cameras in. You'll have to work your charm there as it's him you're going to be following. The hospital wants you alongside someone senior—I guess there's less chance of him making a mistake on national television.'

Erin screwed up her nose. 'I thought it was up to us how we approached it?'

'It is,' Mark assured her. 'You'll just be on the same shift as him.'

Erin nodded relieved. 'When do we start?'

'I've put you straight onto it. Agnes can take over the gym scam from you. She could use a few sessions on an exercise bike, and you can head straight over to the hospital, start getting a feel for the place. Samuel Donovan is on this weekend. We'll film everything we can and then start working on it the following week, see what sort of material we've got. Hopefully it will be a busy weekend at the hospital.'

Erin snapped her notebook shut. 'I hope so, too—not that I wish anyone sick, of course,' she added hastily.

'You're too soft to be a journalist, Erin,' Mark said fondly. 'Now, I know it's not the interview with the Prime Minister you were hoping for...'

'I wasn't.' Erin said, blushing crimson.

'But this could be pretty exciting stuff. I don't need to tell you we're in the middle of an election. This could be political dynamite for both sides and it's going to have your name on the credits.'

Erin stuffed her papers into her bag. 'Don't worry, Mark, this is going to be great, I can just feel it. You won't regret giving it to me.'

'I know I won't. Anyway, I thought I'd come along

for some of the filming myself. Not to check up on you—
it's just that the subject interests me,' Mark said quickly
at Erin's look. He shrugged and smiled placatingly.
'You'll still be in charge.'

Erin rolled her eyes, but conceded. It wasn't as if she
had a choice, anyway.

Across the city in the boardroom at Melbourne City
Hospital the same subject was being discussed, but it was
being greeted with far less enthusiasm.

'First you tell me to not worry, there's an experienced
journalist coming and even though I'm still opposed to
it I start to at least consider the idea. Now you tell me
that he's covering the election instead, and we, or rather
I, are going to be saddled with some unknown journalist
with unlimited access to the department—and you want
my *consent*?' Samuel Donovan threw down his pen on
the polished table. 'Well, no way. Tony Dean would
never agree to this in a million years.'

Bruce Anderson fiddled with his tie, his eyes unable
to meet the direct angry stare being thrown in his direction. 'But as we all know, Tony Dean is on extended sick
leave. You said yourself you didn't want him to be bothered by us with the problems of the department. Now, if
you refuse to agree to this I shall have to contact Tony
myself—he is, after all, the senior consultant.'

He put up a hand as Samuel started to protest. 'I'm
sorry Samuel, but I'll have no choice. You know yourself
the bad publicity the hospital has been getting of late. By
allowing the cameras in, we can at least show the type
of pressure we face and hopefully show some of the good
work we do.'

Samuel pulled a face. 'Do me a favour—do you really
think that this journalist is going to give us a favourable

report? He'll be out for every bit of scandal he can lay his hands on. And leaving aside the poor light it could put us in, what about the patients and their relatives? What could the ramifications be for them, having their trip to the department broadcasted on national television?'

'Everyone will be informed and nothing will be filmed without their consent.'

'As if they'll be in any position to give informed consent.' Samuel stood up. He'd had enough of this ridiculous discussion. 'I have to get back to the unit. We're busy—as usual,' he added pointedly. 'I'll think about it, that's all I can promise.'

Bruce cleared his throat, and dabbed at his forehead with his handkerchief. Samuel wasn't the easiest man to come up against. Not only did he stand at six feet five, he also had the build of a rugby forward and his temper was legendary.

'You've been "thinking" about it for quite long enough. The production team will be here later this morning, you can discuss your fears with them. But *rationally*, please, Mr Donovan. We don't want to give them a bad impression before the cameras even start rolling.'

Samuel turned, his eyes narrowing. 'You mean you've agreed to this charade? How dare you just go ahead? Of all the stupid times to have a film crew! We've got the new residents' rotation starting today—you know what it's like when it's all new junior doctors down there.' He jabbed an angry finger in the air.

'But, then, you don't know, do you? It's not as if you ever make an appearance in the department unless it's to speak to the news reporters, and even then it's only if it's good news. If it's not flattering, you leave it to us to fob them off.' He took a deep breath, mentally exploring his options, but he knew he was beaten. 'What if I refuse to participate? What then?'

'Well…' Bruce took a nervous drink of his water. 'I'll have to ring Tony Dean and discuss it with him. Obviously, I'd rather not upset him at this stage of his convalescence. It was, after all, a very serious heart attack he suffered, the poor man.'

'Don't pretend that you care,' Samuel said from across the room, his deep voice a sharp contrast to the insipid, reedy voice of Bruce. 'We all know what caused Tony Dean's heart attack, and if the department carries on the way it is, his won't be the only one.'

'Which is why we have to embrace this opportunity and use it to our advantage.'

But Samuel wasn't going to be swayed. 'Well, if it all blows up in our faces you can't say I didn't warn you.' He tore his angry dark eyes away from the director and in a more pleasant voice spoke to the secretary, who was pretending not to enjoy seeing her boss being taken down a peg or two. 'Mrs Farrell, can you be sure to document my objection to this in the minutes?'

Mrs Farrell nodded, blushing crimson as she did so. But, then, Samuel Donovan had that effect on most women—not that he appeared to notice. The only thing that held his attention was his work and, as the consultant of Melbourne City Accident and Emergency Unit, that was the one thing there was never a shortage of.

Making her way over to the administration building, Erin tried to quell the butterflies in her stomach. So it wasn't the Prime Minister but finally it was her own big piece, not some fill-in segment before the big news story. Erin was determined she was going to give it everything she had. That was so long as she found the administration wing. The signposts had run out long ago. Scaffolding was up against the wall and red diversion arrows were painted everywhere. With relief she saw a doctor walking towards her. Surely she could ask him? She was after all supposed to have been there five minutes ago. But instead of slowing down as he approached her, he carried on striding purposefully and Erin had to flatten herself against the wall to stop herself from being bowled over.

'Excuse me,' she said angrily, retrieving her bag from the floor.

Samuel Donovan turned, and instantly his expression changed from anger to one of apology. 'I'm sorry, I didn't see you. I've got my mind on other things,'

Erin's heart skipped a beat as she stood up. Surely it couldn't be him? The doctor that had been on the night her parents had been brought in, the same doctor that had taken the time to suture her mother. It might have been ten years ago but every minute detail of that fateful day was etched indelibly on her mind. There was no mistake—it undoubtedly *was* him. His hair was shorter now and the nervousness of youth had gone, but the eyes were the same. Erin searched for something to say, her voice coming out breathless as she fought against the images flashing though her mind.

'Are you on your way to something awful or something?' she asked finally, ever inquisitive.

He smiled at her question and shook his head. 'Actually, I was just escaping from something awful.' He ran a hand through his dark blond hair. 'But I'm sorry. They're renovating, I always forget, and the corridors are a lot narrower.'

'I wasn't looking myself. I'm lost actually. I'm trying to find Admin.'

'You've found it.'

Erin gave a knowing nod. 'That would be right. The whole place is collapsing but there's still the funds to redo Admin.'

Samuel laughed at her perception. 'Who do you have to see?'

Erin fished a piece of paper out of her hessian bag. 'I have to ask for a Dorothy Farrell, at Reception.'

'She's the secretary. They were in a meeting but they were just finishing up.' He glanced at his watch. Normally he would have rushed off there and then but, hell, he could surely spare five minutes to take her to where she was going—he had practically knocked her down after all. 'I'll take you,' he offered, but Erin shook her head.

'I'll be fine, honestly.' She suddenly needed to get away—the memories he was evoking were just too painful. 'If you can just point me in the right direction. I know you must be busy.'

He was busy all right. Monday mornings in A and E were never anything else, and the hand clinic would have already started. But surely they could manage without him for a few more minutes? Why he wanted to help so much he couldn't be sure, but there was something about this fiery young woman with her sparkling eyes too big for her elfin face and spiky hair that softened around her cheeks that had him momentarily distracted.

'Just follow me. It's no big deal.'

She had no choice but to follow him. The width of the corridors didn't allow her to walk alongside him and, anyway, Erin had to practically run to keep up with his long, effortless strides. They turned into a stairwell and her silver sandals clattered noisily as she climbed up behind him. They arrived at the top and Samuel opened the door. Erin peered past him.

'Ah, the potted plants and beige carpets of Admin.

Thank you.' She added, 'It would have taken me for ever to find it.'

'Next time just follow the smell of filtered coffee.'

'I will.' She ducked past him.

Samuel lingered a second. 'Are you here for a job?' he asked, effectively prolonging their brief meeting.

'Sort of. I'm Erin Casey. I'm a television reporter and I'm going to be shooting a documentary on A and E.' She offered her hand, oblivious of the change in his demeanour.

'And you are?' she asked.

'Samuel Donovan. I'm the accident and emergency consultant.'

'Oh.' Her face fell. It would seem she was going to be confronting a lot of ghosts from her past. Erin forced herself to concentrate on the issue in hand. 'Which, from what I've heard, means that you don't like me very much?'

Her huge eyes slowly lifted up and met his, and for a second or two Samuel felt a jolt of recognition and something else he couldn't identify stir within him, until he couldn't even remember what he'd been objecting to in the first place.

He tore his eyes away and looked down at her still outstretched hand. After a moment's consideration he accepted her handshake, trying not to notice how soft and slender her hand felt within his.

'Not you personally,' he said finally. 'Just the whole reality TV concept. It just doesn't sit right with me, not when people are so vulnerable.'

Erin nodded. 'I understand your concerns,' she said. 'But I really don't want to hurt anyone just to get a good story.'

Samuel gave her a doubtful look. 'Isn't that what they all say?'

Erin smiled. 'Sure, the difference is I happen to mean it.'

He watched as she made her way through the door. Closing it, he made his way down the stairwell. Away from her vaguely familiar luminous eyes, at last he could think rationally. Erin Casey was a reporter and out for a story. As soft as her voice was, as kind as her responses to his concerns had been—that simple fact meant that everything he said was on the record. He had the department to think of and, as nice as she seemed, he'd better not forget it. Walking through the heavy black swing doors labelled STAFF ONLY, he saw an ambulance trolley being rushed through to the resuscitation area.

'Good, you're back, Sam.' Fay Clarke, greeted him with a smile. 'The hand clinic will have to wait. They need you in Resus 1.' Samuel nodded as he slipped off his white coat and tied on a plastic apron. The weight of responsibility descended again on his broad shoulders. Funny, when he'd met Erin for a few moments he'd actually forgotten about the place. If she had that effect on him it was all the more reason to be careful. Too many people depended on him—not just with their jobs but with their lives. It was an awesome responsibility and not one he was going to compromise no matter how appealing the distraction might be.

CHAPTER TWO

'WE'RE going to call it *Twenty-Four Hours in A and E*.'
Erin beamed at the gathered staff in the accident and
emergency coffee-room. 'It's got a nice ring to it, don't
you think?'

'Not if it's the start of your shift,' Samuel said dryly,
and everyone laughed. Everyone except Erin. This meeting had been called to officially introduce her and the
team to the A and E staff and it had been anything but
a success. She'd tried everything to inject some enthusiasm about the filming into this cliquish lot. She'd tried
to be nice but she'd been met by a stone wall and un-
derhand comments every step of the way. Erin had had
to find out everything for herself, even down to where
the toilets were. This whole thing was going to be a complete non-starter if she didn't somehow get the staff on
her side.

Erin took a deep breath and ignored his comment.
'Look, I just want to thank you for all coming. The cameras will be around on and off this week, working out
angles and doing a few dummy runs. It will also be good
for you all to get used to having them around so you
don't feel so conspicuous when filming starts. Does anyone have any more questions?'

The gathered staff mumbled among each other as Erin
stood there with a forced smile.

'I just want to be sure that if one of the staff requests
it, you stop filming immediately or leave the area,' Fay
Clarke, the nurse unit manager, said.

Erin hesitated before she answered. For the same reason she felt nervous about Samuel, she couldn't quite meet Fay's eyes. 'As I said, although the board has agreed that we have unlimited access, we won't, of course, film if the patient doesn't give their consent.'

'That wasn't what she wanted to know.' Erin didn't even have to turn her head to recognise from whom that comment had come.

'What Fay was asking was whether you would leave the area if she or one of her staff requested it.' Samuel stared at her directly and she forced herself to smile confidently.

'Of course. As long as it's merited.'

'If one of the nursing staff asks you to leave,' Samuel said in a curt voice, 'then it's merited. End of discussion.'

'Now, hold on a minute.' The smile she had been wearing suddenly disappeared from her face and Erin stood straight, addressing not only Samuel Donovan but the entire room. 'The board has given permission for this. We're not a pack of reporters, waiting outside for a bit of gossip. Like it or not, we're here and if the department's going to gain any value from this entire operation we have to have a bit of mutual co-operation. Sure, if you tell me to leave I will, but if you're telling me to leave constantly and for no good reason, there's not much point in us being here.'

She stared around the room but yet again everyone avoided her gaze.

'Well, if you think of anything else that you want to ask, I'll be around for the rest of the day. Thanks again for coming in.'

Erin packed up as the staff left. 'We'll head off to the waiting room,' Dave, the chief cameraman, said.

'Well, get a few shots of the clock on the wall, and

every time you think of it get a few more. I've a feeling it might come in useful.'

'So you can hang us about our waiting times?'

Erin swung around to be greeted by the hostile face of Samuel Donovan.

'As it would seem the waiting room is where I'm destined to be spending most of my time, I might as well get a memento.' She nodded as Dave and his team headed off.

Once they were alone Samuel walked slowly across the room and sat down in one of the chairs. Stretching out his long legs, he leant back and eyed her carefully. 'I saw how uncomfortable you were with Fay's question,' Samuel said steadily, watching as Erin's eyes blinked rapidly. Suddenly she seemed nervous.

Fay's question had had nothing to do with her nervousness around the woman. But she damn well wasn't going to enlighten Samuel Donovan as to the reasons for her tension. He would just think she was playing for a sympathy vote. He'd made it quite clear that he thought she would go to any lengths to get her story.

'What I'm uncomfortable with,' she said finally, her trained voice, clear and crisp, belying the emotions that had just flooded in, 'is the very real probability that we're going to be asked to leave on the slightest whim.'

'That wasn't what Fay was saying, or me. That was just the way you took it.'

'Well, how did you expect me to take it?' she asked, exasperated. 'I know you didn't want the cameras here in the first place, and I knew there'd be some misgivings from the staff, but not this downright hostility. I've been here since Monday and every time I walk up to someone the talking stops. I'm being treated like a leper.'

'That can be changed.'

Erin looked at him quizzically. 'So this is all your doing?'

He didn't look remotely bothered as he answered, 'Guilty as charged.'

'What did you say to them?'

'To tread with caution.'

'But why? I've already told you I'm not out to hurt anyone.'

'And why on earth should I believe you, Erin?'

For some reason Samuel's comment hit a nerve, but why Erin wasn't sure. By now she was more than used to the inevitable wariness people had when dealing with reporters, the automatic assumption they were about to be misrepresented. Yet coming from Samuel it hurt. And when you were hurt you retaliated.

'So this is going to carry on? That's the game you're playing, is it? The staff are going to throw us out of everything remotely interesting and refuse to talk to me. It's hardly going to make a great story.'

'Then maybe you should pack up and go.'

Erin stared directly at him. 'You don't know me very well, Mr Donovan. As I said, it's hardly going to make a great story, but I was referring to the hospital's point of view. I'll get my story, I just can't guarantee your department will come across in a very favourable light.'

Samuel raised his eyebrows. 'So the kitten has claws after all. I wondered how long it would take for your true colours to surface.'

'It was never my intention to come here and do a hatchet job. I just want to get a true picture of the place and it's proving impossible. Even the roster's been changed.'

'No, it hasn't,' he said irritably. 'What are you talking about?'

Erin took a breath. She knew she was right on this one. 'I had a look through the roster. For the last month there's been only one charge nurse on at night with RNs and ENs, yet this weekend you've got Fay, who's doing days at the moment, also coming onto nights this weekend, plus two extra associate charge nurses. It's a bit of a coincidence, isn't it?' she added for effect, a note of triumph in her voice.

'It most certainly isn't a coincidence,' Samuel answered derisively. 'Though I can assure you the rosters haven't been tampered with for *your* benefit. This happens to be the first week of the new residents' rotation. I need the most senior nursing staff available. And if you'd bothered to go a bit further back with your ''research'', you'd have found that the same thing happens here every six months. Aside from a roving camera crew, and a reporter whingeing that the staff aren't treating her nicely enough, I've also got a new set of doctors to show the ropes to. *Twenty-Four Hours in A and E* might have a nice ring to it, as you say, but if you really intend to stick by me this weekend it might not sound quite so attractive by seven o'clock on Sunday.'

Erin faltered, the façade slipping for a moment. She really wasn't much good at playing the hard-nosed reporter, particularly under his steady gaze. He watched as she hesitated, those stunning eyes suddenly seeming to pale. And suddenly Samuel felt guilty for the hard time he'd caused her over the past couple of days. You had to admire her, though. Despite the cool reception from the staff, despite their refusal to accept her, she had persisted relentlessly, smiling brightly and pretending not to notice—until now that was. Now she looked tired and anything but the hardened reporter out for a story that he had warned the staff about.

'As I said, the staff's attitude can be changed. I just have to say the word.'

'Who are you, the Godfather?' Erin asked angrily, but her temper was more directed at herself for having confronted him without researching the roster properly.

'Around here I am. Look…' He shrugged. 'The nursing staff are the lynchpins here. They make the place work. Get to know them and they're the most amazing bunch of people—warm, funny, extrovert.'

'But they won't let me,' she argued.

'Let me finish. They're also the bitchiest, cliquish lot imaginable. They have to be. It's fifty per cent boredom here and fifty per cent adrenaline. These guys see the worst atrocities and get very little thanks. They rely on each other for moral support. Treat them right and you'll never look back.'

'But I was never going to do anything else.'

Samuel shook his head. 'You don't understand. I'll give you a couple of examples.' He thought for a moment. 'Take Louise—the RN who asked about make-up?'

Erin gave a small laugh. Louise had been hoping for a mobile dressing room.

'Louise takes her appearance very seriously,' Samuel continued. 'She also thinks she's a size eight.'

'So what has that got to do with anything?' Erin asked, bemused as to where this conversation was leading.

'Well, when someone comes in with cardiac arrest and Louise jumps up onto the resuscitation bed to give cardiac massage, where will your cameras be?'

Erin rolled her eyes. 'At the back of the room, no doubt, with a zoom lens—provided we're allowed in, of course.' She thought she saw the tiniest beginnings of a smile at the corners of his lips.

'Exactly. And when your good self and your team review the film, do you really think you're going to care about the embarrassment that will cause Louise? OK, here's another one. One of the RNs is having an affair—I'm not going to tell you which one so don't even ask,' he said quickly as Erin's eyes widened. 'Now, I'm not saying that I approve, because I don't. But the girls chat—what if something untoward comes across on camera? How much damage could that cause? And it's not only the staff but the patients, too. Hell, they might give their consent but they need someone watching out for them as well.'

Erin thought about what he was saying. He had a good point.

'I promise I'll be as sensitive as I can.'

'Uh-oh.' Samuel shook his head. 'I want in. I want to see your work before it goes to air.'

'As if the network's going to allow that. Even the board of directors isn't getting a preview.'

'Surely you could run it by me?'

'No way—you'll edit everything,' she said angrily. 'And anyway, I can't just go chopping bits out here and there—I haven't got that kind of authority.'

'I thought you were co-producer?'

Erin chewed on her nails.

'Look, Erin, I honestly just want to look out for the staff and patients. I know you've got a job to do and I respect that.'

'No, you don't,' she grumbled, and Samuel finally smiled at her petulant face.

She looked up, catching her breath. Suddenly he was the same man she had met in the admin corridor.

'Oh, yes, I do, but you have to respect mine. I run this place, I'm going to be here long after the cameras pack up and go. Give me your word that I can see it *before* it goes to air and I'll tell the A and E crew to treat you as one of the guys. You'll be in for the ride of your life.'

She gave a small nod. 'Do you want it in writing?'' she asked ungraciously.

He looked at her consideringly for a moment and Erin felt the colour in her cheeks mounting under his open scrutiny. The same butterflies that had fluttered at their first meeting seemed to have returned for a second visit.

'No need for that. I trust you,' he said finally.

Despite herself, Erin couldn't quite believe how good those words made her feel. She had to have the final parting shot, though. 'You just want the first view of Louise's *derrière*.'

Samuel laughed. 'You're wasted as a reporter. You should be a casualty nurse.'

Returning from lunch, Erin braced herself for the same frosty reception she had by now grown used to. The smiling faces that greeted her were almost unrecognisable.

'Hi, there, Erin, come over here.' Fay gestured to the nurses' station where the afternoon shift was receiving handover.

'I'll just give the report. You can have a listen, see how we do it, and then Sam and I will give you an in-depth tour of the place. It's better if we both take you around as, no doubt, one of us will be called away.'

Erin nodded eagerly and joined the group of staff around the whiteboard.

'This is the lifeline of the department. Nobody does *anything* without writing it here first.'

'Even in an emergency?'

'No, but as soon as possible after. Look, you see Hilary, the RN, over there?' Fay pointed across to the cubicles. 'Well, she's now moving cubicle six over to

Resus. He'll now be Jo's patient who's down for Resus this afternoon.' She rubbed out the name in the cubicle six area of the whiteboard.

'What bed?' Fay shouted across the department.

'Three,' said an unknown voice.

'So I write his name here in Resus 3's box,' Fay said, doing so. 'And all his investigations and diagnosis. Now, when any results or relatives come, anyone dealing with it knows where the patient is. It also means that cubicle 6 is now free.'

'But not for long?' Erin ventured.

'You're getting the idea,' Fay said, smiling. 'We may look as if we spend half our time staring aimlessly at the thing, but at any given time you can see who's in the department, what their diagnosis is, what the treatment is, what they're waiting to have and the "planned" outcome.'

'Planned?' Erin questioned.

'Well, you know what they say about the best-laid plans? In Accident and Emergency, take that and multiply it by ten, or ten thousand. They can be waiting for a simple X-ray—but who knows what's going to come through the doors? A simple X-ray may suddenly be way down on the list of priorities, for the radiography department as well as the medical personnel and even the porters. Or the patient could be waiting for the last bed in the hospital, but until the patient in the bed is safely out of the hospital doors, who knows what's going to happen?'

'And then we have to wait for the bed to be cleaned,' one of the other nurses said, and Erin heard the note of sarcasm.

'Ah, yes,' said Fay. 'And we all know how long that takes.'

'Because of a lack of domestic staff?' Erin probed, but Fay gave a cynical laugh.

'Sometimes. But the wards are busy, too. They know as soon as they declare the bed, we'll fill it. It doesn't make them too keen to rush to the telephone, so it's generally left to us to keep pestering them.'

'Isn't that the bed co-ordinator's job?' Erin asked, but Fay gave a simple shrug.

'They haven't got the time to make constant manual inspection of the wards for possible beds. They go by their books, the same way we go by the whiteboard. We also use other techniques, of course.'

At that moment the overhead system let out three chimes and everyone stopped what they were doing.

'Medical Emergency Team to Ward 6, please. Medical Emergency Team to Ward 6,' The switchboard operator announced.

A couple of doctors appeared from the screened cubicles and ran out of the department.

'There's one of the techniques,' Fay said, resuming their conversation. 'We'll soon find out the outcome of the medical emergency from the porters or the doctors when they get back. Maybe then we'll find a bed for cubicle 2.' She got a red marker and circled the letters AB on the whiteboard.

'But aren't the beds left a while if someone...' Erin's voice trailed off.

'Dies?' Fay said matter-of-factly. 'You'd better get used to saying it down here.' Fay gave her arm a friendly pat. 'In the old days maybe, but beds are like gold dust here. There's no time to get too sentimental—you have to look after the living.'

Erin nodded and looked at the jumbled words and letters scrawled over the whiteboard. It looked like another language. 'What's AB?' She asked.

'Awaiting bed,' all the staff chorused, and Erin looked up and smiled. She was finally in!

By the time the handover was finished Erin had also learnt that MVA meant motor vehicle accident and CAR meant child at risk. CP meant chest pain and FI meant for investigation. It was another language entirely and one Erin desperately wanted to learn.

'Ready, Fay? I've got half an hour to take Erin around.' Samuel walked up to them.

'We're coming now. I'll be in the department,' Fay told the staff as they walked off.

As they made their way out of the main area Erin turned to Fay.

'I'm sorry about being so evasive earlier. Of course, if either you or one of your staff ask us to get out, we'll do so immediately.'

'Thanks, Erin,' Fay said gratefully. 'I'm not just being difficult. Being a good A and E nurse means being able to read the signs *before* something obvious happens. I'm all for you getting some good shots, but there's a lot more to Accident and Emergency than people with their legs hanging off, as you're about to find out. For instance, a perfectly charming young man may look harmless enough, but if one of our staff recognises that he may be psychotic, well, a camera crew is only going to aggravate things. A simple abdominal pain may be something more sinister or more personal and a lot of patients might not open up too easily. Often even the relatives that are with the patient don't know the full reason why their relative is here, and the nurse may pick up that there's more going on than first appears. That's why it's essential that you leave when we ask, even though it might seem unnecessary at times. Rest assured, if we can keep you there we most certainly will.'

'Thank you,' Erin said, and smiled at the older woman.

'You look familiar,' Fay said. 'I expect I must have seen your face on television.'

Erin shook her head. 'I've never actually got my face on the screen yet, just my voice.'

'But I'm sure I've met you before,' Fay insisted.

Erin felt the beads of perspiration start to form on her forehead but she kept her voice light as she spoke. 'My sister suffers with very bad asthma. We've had to make a lot of trips here in the past. It's probably from then.'

'Perhaps,' Fay said, but she didn't sound convinced.

Samuel carried on walking, seemingly oblivious of the conversation that was taking place.

'Here we are—the main waiting room. This is where patients who aren't bought in by ambulance first present. Everyone is assessed here by the triage nurse.' He pressed a green button and the sliding door opened. 'Here's the ambulance reception area. The same triage nurse assesses the ambulance cases also.'

'She's pretty busy, then?' Erin asked.

'He or she,' Samuel reminded her. 'I thought you were a bit more politically correct than that, Erin?'

Erin ignored his sarcastic comments, instead listening intently to Fay who, with a laugh, took over the explanation. 'And she—or he,' Fay added, shooting a look at Samuel, 'also has to be very observant. Just because a patient has been bought in by ambulance, it doesn't necessarily mean that they're sicker than the ones in the waiting room. The nurse here will be constantly assessing the queue of patients for anyone who looks in difficulty, as well as trying to keep an eye out on patients already waiting.'

Samuel added, 'The nurse takes the details and does a brief assessment, and then the patient is given a grading from one to five. One being the sickest.'

'Like a chest pain?' Erin ventured, but Samuel shook his head.

'One is the number you don't want to get. They don't even stop for assessment. They're straight through to the resuscitation area and it normally means that they're already having lifesaving techniques such as cardiac massage or are requiring immediate lifesaving intervention.'

Erin nodded. 'So what do I have to have to get a two?'

Samuel gave the briefest hint of a smile. 'Well, a chest pain would be a possibility, but even then you might not make it. Category two is for patients that have to be seen immediately in the triage nurse's opinion and possibly they may be put straight into the resuscitation area in case they're about to go off.'

'Go off?' Erin queried. 'You make it sound like a carton of milk left in the sun.'

'Sorry, you'll soon get used to the jargon. About to crash, I mean, or collapse—you'll soon find out.'

'Well, I've still got my chest pain, but the triage nurse doesn't think I'm likely to "go off". Surely I'll get a category three?'

This time he really did smile. 'Not necessarily. Does the chest pain sound cardiac-related, or is it pleuritic? Is it muscular in origin—has there been any fall or recent injury? Have you ever had this pain before?'

Erin stared at him, bemused. 'There really is a lot to think about.'

'That's why I only have very experienced staff on triage,' Fay explained. 'Most of the staff don't like doing it, they want to be out where the action is, but it really is necessary to have a skilled triage nurse. It makes the place run a lot more smoothly.'

'So what happens if I get a category three?'

Samuel carried on explaining. 'Well, category three gets you more or less straight through and probably onto a trolley. Your obs will be done and you'll have a close eye kept on you until a doctor becomes available. Of course, if your condition worsens or the nurse is worried we get you seen straight away. Category four means you're not a priority at the moment and will probably have to wait in the waiting room or maybe in the E-bay, which is like a holding bay for the borderline patients.'

'And if I get a category five?'

He rolled his eyes. 'I just hope you brought a good book to read.'

They made their way through to the resuscitation area. Jo was working quietly, recording observations on the patient that had earlier been brought over to her.

'Everything all right?' Fay asked.

Jo looked up. 'The medics are still stuck with the MET call on Ward 6. I'll have to page them again—he's still got chest pain and he's bradycardic.'

'How many patients can you accommodate in here?' Erin asked.

'We have three adult beds, each with cot sides which can be put up for children or unconscious patients, or patients that are confused or perhaps thrashing about— that type of thing,' Samuel explained as Fay made her way over to the patient. 'But in here there's generally a nurse with them all the time so there's not much chance of them falling off. There's enough equipment and space in here, though, to bring in more trolleys if more than three patients need the room.

'There's also a cot but generally the babies stay on the

bed if they're that sick as the cots don't allow for easy
access. We also have a resuscitation cot in the corner.
Hopefully you won't have to see that being used. It has
an overhead heater to keep the baby warm and all the
oxygen and suction equipment attached. The height of
the cot means that it's ideal for working on a sick baby.'

Erin gazed slowly around the room, listening intently
as Samuel spoke. She was utterly fascinated.

'Generally, we don't allow relatives in here if it's busy,
even if their own relative is stable. We need instant access to all areas and it's hard climbing over people, not
to mention the fact it can be very distressing for the vis-
itors to listen to another person being resuscitated. Of
course, if a child is in here and someone else is very sick
we try to let a parent stay, but even then it depends
what's going on. There's no real constant here. It also
depends what staff are on. Some don't mind relatives
staying, others find it harder to work with an audience.'

'I guess it also depends on the way the relatives are,'
Erin said. 'I mean, if they're calm and sensible I guess
it could help in some circumstances, but if they're over-
wrought—'

'Or drunk,' Fay volunteered, coming over. 'He's still
in a lot of pain, Sam,' she added.

'OK, give him another 5 mg of morphine and tell the
med. reg. to get himself down here or we'll be putting
out an emergency call.'

'It's fascinating,' Erin stated honestly, her eyes slowly
working their way around the room as Fay relayed
Samuel's order to Jo before continuing the tour.

'We put the relatives in here,' Fay said cheerfully,
throwing open a door. 'They're called the interview
rooms. We have three, but sometimes that's not enough.
Other times they can be filled with patients—like an el-

derly lady who doesn't need to have her ears burnt by the drunks in the waiting room, or an anxious child. But generally we try to keep them for sick patients' relatives. We write the patient's name on the whiteboard on the door so we don't give the wrong relatives the wrong news.' She stared as Erin's eyes widened. 'And that's happened a few times, unfortunately.'

'It's very simple, just a table and chairs and a phone. We try to keep it stocked with tissues and there's filtered water.'

She gestured for Erin to follow her in, but Erin stood there, frozen, her feet firmly rooted to the spot.

'Come and have a look,' Fay said brightly.

But Erin could see all she needed to from the door. It was as if she had stepped back in time for a moment. Suddenly she was eighteen again, sitting in that bland room, trying desperately to remember her aunt's telephone number, oblivious of the scratches on her face from the car's broken windows as she comforted her terrified younger sister. It had been Fay who had come in and comforted them both that terrible evening when Samuel had broken the awful news. Fay who had stayed long after her shift had ended, not leaving them until their aunt had come to collect them. Fay who had taken Erin in to see her parents and had held her hand as she'd tearfully said her goodbyes. Ten long years ago, Fay had been slimmer and younger, but the calm compassion she had shown would always be remembered.

'Come on,' Fay said brightly. 'I thought you wanted a guided tour?'

Erin dragged herself back to the present. For a moment she stood there, helpless. Her first instinct was as it had been on that fateful day—to turn on her heel and run out of the department and into the fresh air where the sun was shining and the world was carrying on, oblivious to the tragedy that had unfolded. But instead she just stood there.

It was Samuel who spoke. 'We'll go over to the E-bay.'

Erin looked across, and saw by his eyes that Samuel had finally recognised her, but there was no time for words or explanations as Flynn, the porter, rushed up.

'Fay, Jo needs you in Resus.'

Fay gave an apologetic smile. 'Oh, well, it was good while it lasted. Sorry, Erin.'

Once Fay was safely out of earshot Erin turned shyly to Samuel. 'Thank you for not saying anything, and for remembering, too. I expect you see a lot of tragedies.'

'Too many,' Samuel agreed. 'And I don't recall all the faces, I admit that. I'd go crazy if I did. But...' He paused.

'Tell me,' Erin urged, her need for information, for closure, as prevalent now as it had been back then.

'Well,' he continued slowly, 'it just hit me hard. I know it sounds gauche, but you all seemed so nice, so normal. It kind of hit home the job I was getting myself into. I often thought of you and your sister, how you managed after that awful day.'

Erin shrugged. 'We managed.'

They walked along to the coffee-room and Erin sat down as Samuel poured her a coffee. 'My aunt—you probably wouldn't remember, but she came to the hospital and collected us—had never had children herself. She was a kind woman but the last thing she wanted was two orphans. Anyway, I was eighteen, so I gained custody of my sister Anna, and we just carried on as best we could. It was pretty hard for her, though. She went off the rails a bit.'

'Must have been hard for you, too. Eighteen years old and not only dealing with your grief but all the sudden responsibility.'

Erin nodded. 'It was worth it in the end. Uni was hard, though, everyone out partying while I was forever rushing home and trying to sort out the house and the bills and Anna—she was a full-time job then.'

'How is she now?'

Erin blinked and then her face broke into its usual smile. 'After all the grief she gave me, she's turned out to be the sensible one. She's getting married soon to this terribly conservative lawyer. Anna worries about me now.' She laughed, but Samuel's face was still serious.

'In what way?'

'Oh, nothing serious, just that I don't eat properly and I'm too scatty. I'm a vegetarian and Anna thinks you have to eat meat at least once a day—you know what I mean. I'm into meditation and massage and aromatherapy, Anna's into needlework. We're just chalk and cheese. I think she worries I'm going to end up some sort of hippy, or join a cult or something strange.'

Samuel smiled and gave a small laugh.

'Look, if something comes in that upsets you and you want to talk, just say the word.'

'Thank you,' Erin said simply.

'Sam…' Fay burst into the staffroom. 'Jo's having no luck getting the med. reg. down. I've had a go and it's the same story for me. I think you'd better come—the patients dropped his BP.'

Samuel didn't even attempt to apologise for the expletive that escaped from his mouth as he angrily made his way out of the room.

'Poor med. reg.,' said Erin as the door slammed loudly.

'I wouldn't like to be in his shoes when Samuel gets hold of him.'

Fay just laughed. 'Don't let our Sam upset you when he shouts. He doesn't upset us, we're all far too used to it—not that we don't pay attention to what he's saying or anything. It's just the way it is. Things can get pretty tense around here.'

'What about you?' Erin asked. 'Do you ever lose your temper or get ruffled?'

Fay picked up Samuel's half-drunk coffee and walked over to the sink to rinse his cup.

'I work differently to Sam. He's very passionate, wants everything done *now*. I just try to sort out the chaos and give him what he wants. He's the most amazing doctor, the one I'd want to see if I was coming through the resuscitation doors on a trolley.' She turned and smiled. 'Now it's me who's not answering the question properly. Yes, I have lost my temper down here—twice, to be precise. And on both occasions it was completely and utterly merited, although I still blush just thinking about it. It made Sam's tantrums look like child's play.'

'So I'd better not get on the wrong side of you?'

Fay smiled. 'You're fine. Come on, let's see what's happening out there.'

As they walked, Erin reflected that, despite her earlier hesitancy, she was actually pleased Samuel was going to be around this weekend. In the times she had visited the department because of her sister's asthma, she had been able to keep her mind off the death of her parents by concentrating only on Anna. And she'd succeeded, sort of. But seeing the interview room had been all too real and she braced herself for the carnage she might have to witness at the weekend. It would be nice to have an ally.

As they breezed through the doors, chatting amicably,

the booming voice of Samuel Donovan stopped Erin completely in her tracks.

'Finally, where the bloody hell have you been?'

'We were only a couple of minutes,' Erin said, flustered and shocked at his anger.

Samuel walked over to her, a look of confusion on his face. 'What on earth have they all been saying about me? You didn't think I was talking to *you* like that, did you?'

Erin nodded. 'Well, I have heard you have a bit of a temper,' she said defensively.

Samuel laughed. 'Only for those that deserve it.' He looked over her shoulder at the med. reg. who was beating a hasty retreat into the resuscitation area.

'I'll speak to you later,' he called sharply to the med. reg.'s departing back, and then turned and looked at Erin. 'I may not want you here but that doesn't mean I would shout at you for no reason. I'm not an ogre.'

'I know,' she admitted.

'My only concern is for the patients. If I feel their care is being compromised, I respond as you just saw.'

She understood this—in fact, she actually applauded it. Here was a doctor who cared passionately, who demanded the best at all times for his patients. If he made a noise along the way then so be it. Anyway, it would make for some great action shots. 'Thanks for talking to the staff. This afternoon's been great.'

Samuel nodded. 'I'd better get on—are you coming in tomorrow?'

'No, the camera crew might be in for a while but I'm going to be doing a bit of research and work on the format. I might pop in on Saturday morning.'

Samuel shook his head. 'I'm rostered on from seven on Saturday evening. If you're going to stick with me that means you'll be here until seven p.m. on Sunday. I

suggest you get as much sleep as you can on Saturday—
I know that's what I'll be doing. Of course, there's on-
call beds and we'll grab a few hours when we can. If it's
nothing interesting, I won't wake you up.'

Erin shook her head fiercely. 'I don't care if you're
brushing your teeth. I want to be with you for the full
twenty-four hours.'

Samuel raised his eyebrows. 'I'm allowed to go to the
bathroom by myself, I hope?'

'Not without telling me first,' Erin joked, despite her
crimson cheeks.

'Where do you live?' he asked, and Erin felt a surge
of delight at him asking about her.

'In Camberwell.'

'Nice,' he replied. 'I'm not far from there myself. Do
you want me to pick you up? You won't be up to driving
home by Sunday night, I can guarantee that. I generally
end up sleeping here.'

Erin declined. 'I'll be all right. Thanks, it's nice of you
to be concerned.' Her illusion was quickly shattered.

'I was more worried about getting all the way home,
only to be called in for an MVA caused by you falling
asleep at the wheel. Write down your address, I'll pick
you up.'

But Erin was far too independent to be ordered about.
'I'll be getting here way before seven and, anyway, I'm
quite capable of ringing for a taxi.'

'On a Saturday evening?' he argued. 'You'll be lucky
to get here by midnight. There's a big footy match on at
the MCG—the taxis will be busy.'

Reluctantly Erin scribbled down her address. 'I'll pick
you up around five,' he said, and marched off.

She knew he was suspicious of her, knew he didn't
want her here, but something in his eyes told her that it

wasn't aimed at her personally... Despite his words, she was touched at his concern for her driving, and puzzled, too. After twenty-four hours in this place, why on earth didn't he just get a taxi home if he didn't want to drive? Anyone else would be desperate to escape the place.

Unless, of course, there was no one to go home to. She pondered this for a moment and, closing her eyes for an instant, an image of him coming home after an exhausting shift came into focus. Tired and weary after a draining weekend, coming home to an empty house. The image shifted and a more pleasant picture drifted into the scene—soothing frankincense burning, a welcoming meal on the table and, afterwards, a gentle massage to melt away the tension. Erin opened her eyes abruptly. Where on earth had that come from? That was one story line she most certainly wouldn't be investigating further—the image of Samuel Donovan coming home, coming home to *her*.

CHAPTER THREE

'WHO was that?' Anna asked as she made her way up the garden path. 'Someone from work?'

Erin didn't answer. Instead, she made her way inside to the kitchen and proceeded to open a tin of dog food as Hartley slavered noisily at her feet. 'You're early.'

Anna hung her keys up on the hook by the fridge and poured herself a drink of water. 'Do you want me to do that?' she asked, noticing Erin screwing her nose up as she opened the tin.

'So who was that?' Anna persisted, scraping the food into the bowl as Hartley simultaneously tucked in greedily.

Erin had been hoping to avoid this conversation for a while but, given the pile of brochures left on the bench, it was only a matter of time until Anna worked it out for herself. 'An estate agent,' she said quietly, watching as Anna paused for a moment then stood up.

'Erin, we've been through this. There's no need to do anything. Just because I'm getting married, it doesn't mean things have to change.'

Erin sighed loudly. 'Of course it does, Anna. Look, I know you're not going to throw me out on the street and demand half of what's yours or anything so dramatic, but at the end of the day there are going have to be some changes. Half of this home is yours and rightfully so. We do have to talk about it—I don't even know what your plans are. You and Jordan have as much right to live here as me—'

'We're going to get our own place,' Anna interrupted, 'so you don't have to move out. Look, I know what this place means to you, Erin, and I love it, too. But, to be honest, it just doesn't hold the same feelings for me. I'm ready to move on, to move into my own home.'

'I understand that,' Erin said, 'but if we sold this place you and Jordan could get ahead so much sooner. Mum and Dad would want that. The estate agent gave me a figure.'

She watched Anna's eyes widen in surprise as she relayed the estimated value of the home.

'But it's not all about money, Erin. I know what this place means to you. I know it would break your heart to sell it.'

Erin couldn't answer for a moment. Walking over to the bay window in the lounge, she stood in silence, watching as the automatic sprinkler system spluttered into life. The small black valves popping out from the grass, the familiar hiss and spurt as the water thundered through the system, then sprang forth. The jets of water catching the afternoon sun, casting prisms of colour across the garden. 'The rainbow-making machine' she'd called it as a child. And standing there, watching the soothingly familiar sight, Erin could almost make out two little girls running around the garden—one older and blonder, laughing with delight as she begged the smaller, darker one to join her as she ran, shrieking, through the icy jets. Anna was right. The thought of selling the family home was abhorrent to her.

'Maybe we won't have to sell it,' she said quietly, an idea forming in her mind. 'Perhaps I can get a mortgage and buy you out. Jordan could do all the paperwork.'

'Maybe,' Anna said slowly, but she looked far from convinced. 'It would be a huge mortgage, though, Erin.'

'I should be able to get it. Work's going well, and I'd
have lots of equity or whatever they call it. I mean, I'd
own half of it.' Erin's voice lifted as she realised there
was a way she could keep the house, but Anna still didn't
look too pleased. Ever practical, she pointed out the pit-
falls.

'Erin, it would be a huge commitment. Is that what
you really want?'

'I could take a lodger,' Erin responded quickly. She
was on a roll now. 'Two even. And guess what? My work
did call today—they want me to do some interviews with
the A and E staff and some camerawork of my own. I'm
finally going to get my face on screen. If this takes off,
I'll be in for a nice pay rise.'

All Anna could do was smile at her enthusiasm. 'And
here was me thinking you were sleeping today. Look,
Erin, I'm not going to be a martyr and say that some
money wouldn't be nice, but I don't want it to come at
the expense of your happiness. You're far more important
to me than any lump sum. Let's just forget about it for
a while. You concentrate on work and I'll concentrate on
the wedding.' She looked around the kitchen. 'And clear-
ing this mess up. I can't believe you had an estate agent
in while the place was such a mess.'

Erin laughed. 'Next time I'll get you to clean it up
before they come—that should bump the value up a few
thousand. Who knows? You might be able to afford Paris
for a honeymoon.'

Samuel glanced at his street map and turned into
Wattletree Street. He had known it was an affluent area
but even he managed a low whistle as he drove slowly
down the road, looking out for number seventeen. Maybe
he shouldn't have been so hasty, offering her a lift.

Perhaps there was a rich Mr Erin Casey who would have taken care of that. Gliding to a halt, he parked under a large gum tree and stared at the house for a moment before climbing out of his car. In contrast to the Mercedes and BMWs that were parked outside the other houses, a battered Fiat and an old Alfa decorated the drive. Apart from them, the place oozed old Australian charm, from the huge wattle tree that shaded the garden to the native birds taking a late afternoon dip in the ornate birdbath. It also oozed money. Dodging the sprinklers, Samuel made his way up the path and knocked on the heavy oak door, bracing himself for Erin's husband or boyfriend to answer. Instead, a serious-looking, dark-haired girl answered, introducing herself as Anna, Erin's sister.

For Anna there was no start of recognition when she saw Samuel. After all, she had been much younger when the accident had happened. 'Erin's just upstairs, getting changed. Please, come through.'

He followed her through to the lounge. It was hard to believe they were related, let alone sisters. While Erin was tiny and moved quickly, Anna ambled slowly. And while Erin dressed in flimsy Indian silks and crushed velvets, Anna wore a fitted beige suit. But though her eyes were as brown as Erin's were green, she had the same easy smile.

'Can I get you a drink?' she offered.

'No, thanks, we'll be going soon.'

Anna laughed. 'I wouldn't be so sure. Ever since Erin's work rang and told her she was going to appear in the report she's been pulling everything out of her wardrobe. Didn't you hear the screams of frustration as you drove down the street?'

Samuel found himself smiling back. 'In that case, I'll have a coffee, thanks—white with one.'

Two coffees and a packet of Tim-Tams later, Erin breezed into the lounge room. 'You're here already? But it's only just on five.'

Samuel stood up as she entered. 'You look nice,' he offered, noting the subtly rouged cheeks and the darkened lashes framing her vibrant eyes. She was wearing a mint green shift dress that bought out her vivid eyes, and around her slender neck hung a huge green crystal. Erin followed his gaze, and lovingly picked up the stone between her fingers.

'It's green calcite,' she explained seriously. 'It's supposed to promote order and help me to assimilate and retain information.'

Samuel was about to say how it matched her eyes but, realising with a jolt that his comment might come across as inappropriate, instead he gave a thin smile and responded nonchalantly, 'It matches your dress.'

Erin looked down and feigned surprise. 'What, this old thing? So it does. Isn't that a coincidence? It was the first thing I grabbed out of the cupboard. I took your advice and slept most of the day.'

'Glad to hear it.'

Erin, however, wasn't paying attention. 'Why are there never any pens in this place? I had three here this morning,' she moaned loudly, as she rummaged through the pile of papers on the bench.

'Glad to see the crystal's working,' Samuel said dryly, to Anna's open amusement. He picked up his keys. 'Can I just use your telephone? My mobile's battery is flat and I want to let the hospital know I'm on my way.'

Still smiling, Anna directed him to the hall. As he went out Anna grabbed Erin's arm, and for once her usual reserve was gone. 'Erin, why didn't you tell me he's absolutely gorgeous?'

But Erin was far too thrown by her instant attraction to Samuel Donovan to add fuel to the fire, so instead she answered dismissively, 'Don't be fooled. When I first met him I thought the same, but he's got the most foul temper. He can't stand me and doesn't want the cameras there—he's the one I was telling you about. And, anyway, my horoscope warned me to beware of hostile adversaries and not be taken in by their false charms.'

But Anna wasn't going to hear a word against him. 'That,' she said, pointing to the door, 'is a good man. I wouldn't mind spending twenty-four hours cooped up with him.'

'Anna Casey, you're practically a married woman,' Erin said, laughing. 'What would Jordan say if he heard you?'

'All I'm saying is that if you ever get fed up with reporting, maybe you should consider a career in nursing or medicine. And I don't care what your horoscope said. Maybe it was referring to the estate agent. Samuel Donovan is a decent guy.'

Waving back at Anna a few minutes later, Erin leant back in the plush leather seats.

'Nice car,' she observed out loud, but Samuel didn't respond.

Erin picked up a pile of CDs from the dashboard and after a brief flick through promptly returned them.

'Nothing take your fancy?'

'The radio will be fine,' she answered, leaning back and watching as he glided the car through the rush-hour traffic.

'Your sister seems nice,' he said finally, and Erin was relieved that he'd broken the silence.

'She said the same about you.'

'A woman of good taste.' He turned and looked at her.

Trying desperately to ignore the sudden influx of butter-flies that had invaded her stomach, Erin fiddled with the air-conditioning.

'Anna told me she'd just got engaged,' he continued.

'That's right,' Erin replied lightly. 'We were supposed to be going out with Jordan's family tonight to celebrate. Until this came up,' she added.

'What's he like—Jordan?'

Erin chewed her nail as she thought. 'He's very clever. He went to Scotch College and studied law at Melbourne Uni. He's going to make a name for himself—he's doing very well.'

Samuel glanced over. 'I didn't ask for his résumé. I meant, what's he *really* like?'

Erin cast him a sideways glance then rolled her eyes as she answered. 'Condescending and painfully boring, but that's between you and me.'

For a second she thought he was about to laugh, but instead he gave her just the briefest of smiles before asking, 'Have you got a blueprint for this weekend?'

'Not really,' Erin admitted. 'We're going to get as much on film as we can and then see what we've got. Even I've realised now how unpredictable A and E is. We'll probably try to follow a couple of patients through. I want to film the nurses' handover, which will give the viewers a good idea of what's in the department.'

Samuel nodded briefly as she chatted away, but his eyes stayed on the traffic ahead.

'I've spoken to Fay about it,' she continued, 'and as much as possible the nurses are going to refer to the patients by their cubicle number to help with confidentiality.'

Sam seemed to like that and murmured his approval. Briefly he turned. 'So, are you looking forward to the

weekend or is it simply all in a day's work for you? I
expect you've seen a few sights in your time?'

Erin stretched her legs out in front of her. 'Not really,'
she answered truthfully. 'I mean, after a couple of glasses
of Chardonnay I can glam it up a bit, but in all honesty
I haven't exactly cracked any big stories. This weekend
is my big break.'

'Really?' He pushed the gear lever into fifth. 'So what
were you working on before this came up?'

'A dodgy gym that's supposedly pushing steroids. I've
been covering it for two weeks.'

'And are they?' he asked, genuinely interested.

'Probably, but not while I'm around. I've spent the last
fortnight pedaling away and pumping iron, and the most
scandalous thing I've come up with is that the canteen
assistant is filling the decaffeinated coffee-jar from the
regular caterer's tin.'

'And will you expose them?' His voice was serious
but Erin heard the tinge of humour and played along.

'I doubt it. I'd shatter too many illusions—all those
exercise freaks thinking they were getting an adrenaline
rush from exercise, only to find out the coffee wasn't all
it first appeared. I just couldn't do it.'

For a second she detected the hint of a smile on his
deadpan face.

'They've put my good friend Agnes onto it. The
thought of her stuck on a treadmill for five hours a
day…well, let's just say I reckon she'll be grateful for
the steroids and keep quiet—she needs all the help she
can get. I doubt the news team will be getting much of
a story.'

And finally for the first time since she'd met him, Samuel broke into a laugh and Erin—whether it was because
it was so infectious, or the thought of poor Agnes pump-

ing away in her cycles shorts—found herself laughing with him.

Easing into a parking spot, he pulled out his wallet, saying, 'I'll be back in a moment.' He returned with a huge green box which, without a word, he promptly deposited on Erin's knee.

She couldn't resist a peek. 'Cheesecake, yum.' Samuel didn't respond.

They drove in an uneasy silence until they reached the hospital. Always the gentleman, he opened the door and retrieved the cheesecake, leaving her to drag along her bag.

'What on earth have you got in there?' he asked as she struggled with her bag.

'Just a toothbrush and my pyjamas, a change of clothes—that sort of thing.'

Watching her stride into the path of an oncoming ambulance, its siren muted but its lights blazing, he hauled her back. 'Just keep your eyes and ears open,' he said sternly.

'I intend to.' Erin answered, oblivious of the disastrous situation he had just diverted. 'Don't worry about me.'

Samuel rolled his eyes. It would, after all, make a great story—the news reporter mown down in the ambulance bay—but for reasons he didn't even want to explore, he felt duty bound to somehow protect her, despite his misgivings about the whole saga.

'Easier said than done,' was all he muttered as he waved apologetically to the bemused paramedics. 'Easier said than done.'

As she entered the A and E department Erin was almost knocked sideways by the wafts of scent that greeted her—it was like walking into a perfume department. The faces that greeted her were equally unrecognisable, with heavily mascara'd eyelashes and reddened lips. Erin stifled a smile—after all, hadn't she herself spent an hour tarting up?

Samuel obviously read her mind. 'Don't worry, make-up doesn't last long around here. They'll be back to their old selves in no time.'

What was more worrying was the self-conscious way in which the staff were conducting themselves. The camera crew had been around for days now but the staff knew that tonight it was for real. Again Samuel stepped in.

'I don't want to intrude, I'm sure you know best and everything, but maybe if you wore theatre greens you wouldn't be so conspicuous. It's worth a try.'

Erin looked glumly at her dress. It would have looked so sophisticated on screen but, still, the story had to come first.

With a grumbling nod she accepted the linen he handed her.

'Should I wear one of those turban things?' she asked.

Samuel gave her a thin smile. 'Not unless you're intending to operate. If you are, please, at least have the courtesy to let me know first.'

Opening a door, Erin tried to appear as if she was listening as he continued, 'Not the Wentworth Hotel, but this humble room can look just as luxurious by four in the morning. What's wrong?'

'Nothing,' Erin replied, rather too brightly. How could she tell him that standing so close in this the tiniest of rooms was doing the strangest of things to her? She gave a bright smile and hoisted her bag on the bed.

'This will be fine. I've stayed in far worse conditions when I've been on assignment,' she said in what she hoped was a mysterious voice.

'Really?' She was sure he was laughing at her. 'Then I'll leave you to get changed.'

Slowly Erin unpacked, putting her dental floss and toothbrush and paste in a glass by the sink. She laid her notes on the bedside table and set her alarm clock out. An old hospital locker held the rest of her things apart from her toiletry bag which, after a moment's deliberation, she placed on top of the locker. She was getting worked up about nothing, she chided herself. She was a reporter on assignment, and Samuel was her subject— she was bound to find him interesting!

Changing at lightning speed in case he came back, she grimaced as she looked down at the baggy theatre greens swamping her body. She was going to look a fright on television. Jumping onto the bed, she eyed herself in the small mirror above the sink. They weren't too bad after all—in fact, she actually quite liked them she thought, turning around to examine her rear. So long as nobody mistook her for a doctor. She laughed then yelped in horror as there was a knock at the door, which immediately opened.

Mortified, she stood helpless on the bed as Samuel stood at the door. He was definitely laughing at her now. 'When you've finished admiring yourself, I thought I'd take you over to the staff.'

Her skin still stinging with the heat of embarrassment, Erin made her way out. The waiting room was already half-full. Signs were up, warning people of the filming that was taking place, and the triage nurse and receptionist were also explaining what was happening as patients were being admitted.

Dave gave her a wave as she walked through and came over.

'Make sure you film the waiting-room clock at seven,

I don't care what's happening elsewhere, and I'll interview a couple of patients that register at that time.'

Dave nodded. 'You're going to be in the shot, aren't you?'

'Not too much. I want this to be about the patients. Maybe get a couple of shots of me and I can decide later whether or not to keep them in, but in the main keep the camera on the patients. There's going to be a lot going on. If I see anything I want I'll obviously call you, but just get as much as you can yourself.'

Dave nodded cheerfully. He had always liked working with Erin, she wasn't a prima donna who thought she knew best all the time. For the most part she left the camera team to do their own thing, relying on their experience.

'Come and have a look at this.' He had a mischievous glint in his eye and Erin followed him through the unit with a smile.

Setting up his camera he panned across the department, Erin knew he wasn't filming, just setting up, and she watched patiently. Nothing seemed to be happening. The department was quiet compared to the waiting room. A blond-haired doctor strode down, looking very full of his own self-importance, and Dave let out a low chuckle.

'Here he comes. It's like a bee to honey. As soon as I look like I'm filming, he appears. The nurses said he's a surgical consultant, who you normally don't see down here for dust. I haven't the heart to tell him we haven't started filming yet.'

The blond doctor saw her smiling and made his way over.

'I thought I'd better come and introduce myself. I've already had a word with your director. You'll be seeing me a lot over this weekend. I'm Jeremy Foster, the surgical consultant on for this weekend.'

Erin accepted his handshake. 'I'm Erin Casey and this is Dave, the senior cameraman.'

Jeremy held onto her hand far longer than was necessary. 'As I've said, I'll be around but if you do want to follow a particular patient more closely I'd be only too happy to allow you to film up in Theatre. It might be a good story. You know, a bit more in-depth.'

Erin stifled a laugh. 'That's terribly kind of you, but we're actually going to be concentrating on A and E.'

'Oh, well, just a thought. I'll see you around, no doubt.'

'No doubt about that,' Erin muttered as he walked off.

Samuel walked up to them. 'How are you doing?'

'We're being made very welcome. Jeremy Foster just invited us up to film in Theatres. We didn't accept,' she added hastily as she watched his eyes darken. 'I know we haven't got approval for that and anyway, as I said to Jeremy, we want to concentrate on A and E.'

Samuel gave her a relieved smile. 'Just don't go getting stomach pains this weekend or he'll be whipping your appendix out in the middle of the nurses' station if it means he can get on television.'

'I'd worked that one out for myself,' Erin said, laughing. 'But thanks for the warning.'

Mark came up, having arrived to see the start of the filming. 'It's ten to seven,' he warned. 'A taxi has pulled up with an old lady inside. By the time she gets registered it will be seven, so let's start with her.' He nodded to Dave. 'You'll get a shot of the clock?'

Samuel and Dave both rolled their eyes. 'No worries,' Dave said as Samuel made his way into a cubicle.

Erin and the team went through to the waiting room.

For a second she stood there, taking it all in. This was her chance. She felt a surge of excitement as her adrenaline kicked in. They'd talked about it for long enough—now it was time for action.

CHAPTER FOUR

'I'M SORRY to cause such a fuss.' Elsie White looked flustered as she rummaged through her handbag for her purse. With shaking hands she undid the clasp. 'How much do I owe you, young man?'

But the taxi driver shook his head. 'No worries, love. You just make sure they fix up your leg good, and if you need a taxi home, give them my number. I'll make sure you get there safe and sound.'

'That's most kind of you, but really I'd rather pay.' With her trembling hands Elsie unwrapped a huge wad of notes.

'Lord help us,' the taxi driver yelped. 'She's got her life savings with her.'

Vicki, the triage nurse, smiled calmly. 'Put your money away, Elsie. I'll get Security to come and put it in the safe for you. I just need your Medicare card if you've got it with you.'

Elsie carried on going through her bag.

'Don't show that on television,' Vicki warned. 'A lot of old people keep their savings at home, and I'd hate her to get a visit from some undesirables because of this.'

'Absolutely,' Erin agreed, and watched as Vicki made her assessment.

'What happened, Elsie?'

'I fell, silly old fool that I am. I was trying to change a light bulb.'

'Did you have a dizzy turn?' Vicki asked, but Elsie shook her head.

'No, dear, I just missed my footing, coming off the stool. I've cut my leg badly. I tried to stop the bleeding myself but I couldn't. I'm sorry to be such a nuisance.'

Vicki put on some gloves and gently peeled away the teatowel wrapped around the elderly woman's leg. 'A nuisance is the last thing you are. Why didn't you call an ambulance, Elsie? That's a nasty gash you've got there.'

'They're far too busy to be worrying about an old fool like me.'

'Elsie, I won't have you talking like that. You should see some of the fools that the ambulances do pick up— you're an absolute pleasure.'

'Will it need stitches?' Elsie asked, as Vicki gently placed a large wad of Melonin and Combine on the cut and then applied a bandage. 'I'm not sure. Maybe a couple of deep ones, but you've got that very thin skin that tears easily. The doctor will need to have a good look. Did you hurt yourself anywhere else?'

'No, dear, just my leg. Such a nuisance—I was hoping to do some gardening tomorrow.' Vicki persisted with her questions but Elsie was adamant that it was all the result of a simple accident.

Erin watched as Vicki typed in her details, trying to second guess what category the elderly lady would be given.

'How come she's a three?' Erin asked, surprised by the number Elsie had been allocated. 'It just looks like a simple cut.'

Vicki smiled. 'What would you have given her?'

Erin shrugged 'A four or even five.'

'Possibly a four,' Vicki agreed, 'but five is really for people who've had a vague earache for a week or something that should have been dealt with by their own GP.

Elsie is a genuine accident and emergency patient, and clinically she does fit the criteria for a category four, but...' She thought for a moment. 'Well, she's an old lady and very proud. Did you see how she'd put on her lipstick to come here? What a darling...' Vicki gave an apologetic smile. 'Sorry, I'm going off the subject. Well, most people would call for an ambulance, whereas Elsie called for a taxi. It's nothing I can put my finger on, but she obviously doesn't like to make a fuss. I just get a feeling she's not giving us the full story. If I put her at a three she'll probably get onto a trolley and at least she'll have a set of obs done.' Vicki shrugged. 'I'm just an old softie. I hate old ducks like that sitting in the waiting room, and Elsie White is a bit of a cutie. She reminds me of my grandmother.'

Elsie was wheeled through, and after she'd been undressed and placed into a hospital gown as white as the straggly hair on her head Erin and the team joined her, watching quietly as the nurse took some obs. Erin noticed the faintest hint of a frown as Sharon took the old lady's blood pressure, pumping the cuff up and down a couple of times till she was sure of the result.

'Your blood pressure's a bit low,' she said finally.

'It always is,' Elsie said defensively. 'That's better than it being high, isn't it?'

'Now, how about you tell me exactly what happened?'

'But I've already told the nurse out there. I tripped, changing a light bulb, and hurt my leg.'

'You didn't go dizzy?' Sharon persisted.

Erin grinned as the old lady replied curtly, as if she were talking to a child, 'As I've already said, no, dear, I didn't go dizzy. Now, can someone, please, sort out my leg?'

But the nurse carried on with her questions, not remotely fazed by Elsie's tone. 'Have you had any chest pain today, Elsie?'

Elsie fiddled with the blanket. 'It's just indigestion. I had a scone for afternoon tea and it's just not sitting right.'

'I bet you didn't tell the triage nurse that.'

Elsie looked a little shamefaced. 'It's really nothing to be concerned about.'

'I'm paid to be concerned,' Sharon said in a no-nonsense voice, but her eyes were kind. 'You just wait there, Elsie, while I go and get the portable ECG machine.'

'All this fuss,' Elsie muttered as the nurse left the cubicle. Erin smiled at her. She liked this feisty old lady.

'Have you ever been to A and E before?'' Erin asked.

'Never, and I have no intention of coming back. Not that the girls aren't nice, of course, but they make such a fuss. They're going to get security guards to take my money off me, you just watch.'

'Why don't you put it in the bank?'' Erin asked, even though she knew couldn't use this conversation for the show.

'So that they can take all my money and give me some little plastic card back that I can't even use? No, thank you very much.'

Sharon returned with the ECG machine. 'I'm just going to do a trace of your heart, Elsie. It doesn't hurt—I just have to put a few straps around your wrists and ankles and attach some leads to your chest. It looks far worse than it is. You won't feel a thing.' She rummaged around the trolley. 'There's no red dots. I'll be back in a second and then perhaps you could wait outside. I'll need to pull her gown down,' she said to the camera crew.

'Sure,' Erin replied amicably. The last thing she

wanted to do was cause Elsie any embarrassment. Sharon set off to get the equipment that was missing and Erin addressed the elderly woman.

'We'll leave you to have this test, Elsie, and then if it's all right with you we'll pop back.'

But Elsie didn't answer. She was lying back on the pillows and Erin watched in horror as Elsie's face seemed to go all floppy, her eyes rolling back in her head.

'Elsie!' Erin called urgently. 'Oh, no!' She turned to Dave who was still filming and, pushing the curtain to one side, tried to call out for help.

'In here,' she croaked, but the words stuck in her throat. Seeing Sharon walking towards them, she beckoned her over, watching with relief as Sharon read the urgency in her actions and started to run.

'Elsie,' Sharon called, her voice loud and urgent. 'Elsie, can you hear me?'

Slamming her hand against a red button on the wall, she let down the head of the trolley and felt around Elsie's neck for a pulse, hastily slipping an oxygen mask over her darkening lips. The room suddenly filled with nurses and doctors. Samuel took charge.

'What happened?' His voice was deep and calm.

'She just went off,' Sharon explained as Samuel kicked the brakes of the gurney. 'She's got a faint pulse.'

'Let's get her over.' Suddenly the trolley was being wheeled at lightning speed across the department. Erin hesitated for a second then followed. Entering Resus, she took her agreed place at the end of the room and watched as the team of nurses and doctors set to work on Elsie, attaching leads to her chest as they wrapped a tourniquet around her skinny arm.

Samuel slapped the back of her hand to bring the veins up and in seconds he'd inserted an intravenous line. He looked up at the monitor saying, 'She's in sinus rhythm, and her sats are coming up.'

Elsie started moving about the trolley, groaning and thrashing about, pulling at the oxygen mask.

'Leave it on for the moment, Mrs White. You've just had a bit of a turn but you're all right now. I'm Samuel Donovan, the accident and emergency consultant.' He turned to Sharon as he was handed an ECG tracing. 'So what's the story?'

'Eighty years old, presented to the department via a taxi with a lacerated leg. She said she tripped, insisted it was just an accident. She finally admitted she'd had chest pain since this afternoon and I was just about to do an ECG when she went off.'

'Were you with her?''

Sharon shook her head. 'I'd just gone to get some red dots. Erin was with her.'

Samuel looked over. 'Did she complain of chest pain or anything?'

Erin shook her head dumbly. She still couldn't speak.

Dave, who had carried on filming throughout, answered for her. 'She seemed fine and then she just slumped back, Doctor. She didn't say anything.'

Samuel carried on studying the trace as he listened. 'She had a pulse when you got to her?'

Sharon nodded. 'Irregular, though, and bradycardic.'

Samuel nodded. 'She's had an anterior MI—I'll give her some morphine for her pain. Where the hell are the medics? Someone let them know, I hope?'

'They're stuck up on the wards with a patient,' one of the nurses replied.

'Well, what do they think Mrs White is? Tell them to send someone down *now*, or else I'll come and fetch them myself. In the meantime, let's get X-ray round for a portable chest.'

Erin watched the activity, mesmerised. Looking down, she saw that her hands were trembling violently. She simply couldn't believe that just a few moments ago she had been talking to Elsie with seemingly no hint of what lay ahead. Samuel looked over and caught her eye.

'All right?' he mouthed, and she nodded. With a slight frown he came over. 'Come outside. They're going to do an X-ray and one of the nurses will stay with her.' Once outside the resuscitation room he looked at her more closely. 'You're as white as a sheet,' he commented. 'Haven't you seen anything like that happen before?'

Erin shook her head. 'Only on television. Like I said before, most of my jobs have been pretty conservative.' She glanced anxiously over to the gurney. 'She'll be all right, won't she? I mean, I know she's old and that but she just seemed so independent.'

Samuel didn't reply straight away, and when he did his voice was solemn. 'I can't say, Erin. We'll do our best for her but, as you've said, she's old. It's an eighty-year-old heart we're dealing with. We'll do everything we can, of course, but...'

Erin nodded. The sting of tears were starting to burn and, despite her best efforts to hide them, Samuel noticed.

'I'm sorry,' she said angrily, wiping away a tear. 'You must be wondering how I'm going to survive the next twenty-four hours if I'm going to blub every five minutes. I just panicked when I saw her and I didn't know what to do.'

But he didn't seem remotely fazed by her tears. 'And why would you?' he asked reasonably. 'You're a reporter, not a nurse. What did you do?'

Erin swallowed hard. 'Dave has to carry on filming

whatever happens, so I just ran out and tried to find someone—and then I saw Sharon.'

'Next time something like that occurs, just hit the
emergency button. It doesn't matter if it's a false alarm.
Like Agnes, we can all do with the exercise.' Erin managed a smile, touched that he'd remembered the details
of their conversation and also touched at his efforts to
make her feel better.

'And as for your tears,' Samuel continued, 'there's
nothing wrong with a bit of emotion, especially if you're
not used to seeing this sort of thing. It would have been
a bit of a shock. I bet if you went out to triage now,
Vicki wouldn't be the happiest you've seen her.'

'Really?' Erin asked, surprised. 'But she must be used
to this sort of thing happening all the time.'

'Doesn't stop it hurting, though, and apparently she
took a bit of shine to Elsie, according to Sharon. A and
E nurses and doctors build up a rapport very quickly with
their patients—well, the good ones anyway—and some
you just take an instant liking to.'

Erin knew all about instant rapport. Looking up, she
saw he was smiling gently at her. 'I felt a bit like that
about Elsie, too,' Erin commented, feeling better about
the way she'd reacted. 'You just knew as soon as she
spoke that she was a real old character.'

Samuel touched her arm briefly. 'Look, go and grab a
coffee or a glass of water and take five.'

'I can't,' Erin argued. 'It's only half past seven. If I'm
going to be disappearing every time something sad happens…'

But Samuel interrupted. 'I bet Sharon's making Vicki
a coffee now, and then she'll take it over to Triage and
give her an update on Elsie's progress so she can give
Vicki a couple of minutes to talk about Elsie. That's what

I was saying about the nurses here depending on each other. This place is like a field of unexploded land-mines—it takes a huge team effort to get through. If having a cuppa and a chat get you through then go for it.'

The resuscitation doors slid open and the radiographer popped his head out. 'All clear.'

With a brief nod Samuel made his way back into Elsie.

Coffee would have to wait. Erin's attention was instantly diverted as Mark appeared, looking excited. 'Come out to the waiting room, Erin. There's a bit of action going on.'

Erin followed quickly. At the triage desk an angry man was waving a bandaged arm at Vicki.

'I was told I was next on the list, but I've been sitting here for two hours in pain. I came in by ambulance—why haven't I been seen?'

Vicki responded calmly to the irate man. 'Your injury is two days old, Mr Nesbitt. We have to prioritise, and unfortunately that can mean a long wait.'

'So why did that old biddy with a cut leg get taken straight in? She came in by taxi, it can't be that serious. Just because she's old she gets seen straight away! Well, I've got somewhere important to go tonight. I want to be seen *now*.'

Vicki's voice remained calm despite the provocation. 'As I've explained, emergencies take priority. Now, if you'll just take a seat.'

But he wasn't going to be placated. 'Why was that old woman seen first?' he demanded loudly. 'It's a disgrace.' He turned to the cameras. 'I hope you're getting all this.' He banged his fist against the safety glass separating the nurses from the waiting room. 'I want to see a doctor now!'

'Right, that's it,' Vicki said, and Erin knew she was

pressing the distress alarm under the triage nurse's desk. Within a couple of moments two burly security guards appeared.

'Everything all right, Sister?' they asked immediately, walking over to the irate patient.

'I was just attempting to explain the reason for this gentleman's delay but he doesn't seem too keen to listen to my explanation. Perhaps you can do a better job.'

Mr Nesbitt didn't look quite so irate now. 'There was no need to call Security,' he insisted. 'I only punched the glass. I'd never have laid a finger on you.'

Vicki viewed him distastefully from behind the partition. 'I wasn't prepared to take that chance, Mr Nesbitt. Now, if you'd be so good as to have a seat, we'll get you seen as soon as we can.'

'How long has he been here?' Erin asked Mark. 'I can't remember him from before.'

'Exactly,' Mark said. 'He's only been here half an hour.' He turned to Dave, but Dave was ready for him.

'Don't worry, I got a shot of the clock.'

Erin looked up. 'I feel like we've done a night's work and it's still not even eight o'clock.'

Erin made her way through the ambulance reception area to Vicki. 'Are you all right?' she asked.

Vicki looked up from the computer. 'Sure, why?' She watched as Erin nodded in the direction of the waiting room. 'Oh, you mean Mr Nesbitt?' She let out a low laugh. 'That was nothing. You wait till the pubs start turning out.'

'It didn't upset you?' Erin asked, surprised at how little it appeared to have bothered Vicki.

'Not really. Annoyed would be more of an apt description. You've got absolute honeys on the one hand who don't call an ambulance when they really need one and their only concern is not to make too much fuss, and then you have people like him who use the ambulance like a free taxi service for something as trivial as a wrist he sprained two days ago.'

'It's only sprained?' Erin said, the surprise evident in her voice.

'I think so. There's no deformity and he's having no trouble moving it as he so clearly demonstrated. I told him when he arrived that he probably wouldn't be X-rayed tonight. Most likely he'd be asked to come back in the morning—that is, if the doctor even thinks he needs one.'

Erin's eyes widened. 'So he's going to sit here for goodness knows how long just to be told to come back tomorrow?'

Vicki shrugged. 'Probably.' At that moment her attention was diverted as a woman ran into the department.

'Help me.' She was carrying a toddler who was wearing only a nappy, and the child was crying as loudly as her mother. 'I think she stopped breathing,' the woman screamed. 'In the car on the way here. Help us.' Vicki leapt from her stool and with a flick of a large switch opened the ambulance reception doors, hastily making her way over to the woman. Erin braced herself and followed, half expecting to see Vicki run into the resuscitation area with the baby. Instead, she led the shocked woman straight through to the paediatric area.

Dave, seeing the action, made his way over.

'Just lay the babe here. What's her name?' Vicki asked. 'It's all right, I've got it,' she added to Gemma, the other nurse, who was tied up with another small child.

'Nicola,' the woman sobbed.

'And what's yours?' Vicki asked calmly.

'Rita,' she said. 'Is she all right? Is she going to be all right?'

Vicki spoke as she took the toddler's temperature. 'She's fine. Take a couple of big breaths and calm down, you're scaring Nicola. Try and tell me what happened.'

Rita took a few deep breaths and in a trembling voice told how Nicola had been unwell all day. 'I took her to the GP and she said it was just a virus, but Nicola just kept screaming tonight and getting hotter and hotter. I didn't know what to do so in the end I put her in the car and brought her up here. Just as I parked I turned and she started shaking. Her eyes were rolling and I thought she was dead. She's all right, isn't she?' Rita begged again.

Vicki put her arm around the mother. 'She's fine. She's got a very high temperature and it looks as if she may have had a febrile convulsion. Babies aren't able to control their temperatures as well as adults and when they get too warm some babies have a fit. It's very frightening to watch but she's settling now. We'll get the doctor straight in to see her.'

Erin looked on, awestruck. Vicki was superb, reassuring the terrified woman and gently sponging the baby with a damp facecloth. 'When did she last have some paracetamol?' Vicki asked.

'An hour ago, but she was sick straight after.'

Samuel was standing at the foot of the cot with Clint, one of the junior doctors. He smiled briefly and introduced himself. Then he asked, 'Has Sister explained about the cameras here?'

Rita looked around and for the first time realised she was being filmed.

'We didn't really get time,' Vicki explained to Samuel. 'I'll have a word in a moment.'

Samuel nodded. 'What's her temp?'

'Forty point one. She vomited after Mum gave her some paracetamol.'

'OK, give her 125 mg of paracetamol PR and keep on with the tepid sponging.' He turned to Rita. 'Sister's just going to give her a paracetamol suppository to help bring down the temperature, and I'm going to examine your daughter. Why don't you pop her on your knee?'

Calmer now Rita picked up her child. 'Can I give her a drink?'

'Let me just have a look at her first,' Samuel said as he proceeded to examine Nicola. His voice was soft and reassuring and as he did his examination he explained to Clint what he was looking for.

'She's pretty miserable, she's got a slight rash that looks viral,' he observed. He pushed the baby's head gently forward. 'I'm looking for any signs of neck stiffness.' Producing a pen torch, he shone a light into her eyes. 'No photophobia,' he said to Clint, then smiled reassuringly at Rita.

'You don't think she's got meningitis, do you?'

'At the moment we have to consider all possibilities. Her chest is clear and her ears look fine. Her throat's a little bit red but not enough to account for such a high temperature. It's more than likely it's something viral, but we do need to check her out properly. I'm going to get Sister to put some cream on her hands and arms that will numb the area and we'll do some blood tests. I'll also ring the paediatrician and ask whoever's on to come and take a look at her.'

'How long will it take?' Rita asked.

'Hard to say. It will be a while until we get the bloods back but I think you're going to be here some time—they may want to do some further tests.'

'Like...?' Rita asked.

'Let's just wait and see, shall we? At least here we can keep a close eye on her. The night staff are just coming on, so the nurse who'll be coming on duty here will come and introduce herself. But in the meantime, if anything happens you just call out—the nurses' station is just outside.'

Erin walked out with him. 'Do you think Nicola does have meningitis?'

'It's a possibility, and it's something every doctor considers when they examine an unwell child. We dread it as much as anyone does. But in this case, no, I don't think so. I expect the GP is right and she's got a nasty viral infection.'

'Why wait to do the bloods? I mean, if she's sick, wouldn't it be better to get the bloods done straight away?' Erin asked. 'Just a question—I'm not criticising,' she added quickly, but Samuel gave her a small smile to show no offence had been taken by her query.

'It's a good question. Look, if it was Clint on his own, I'd probably play on the safe side and tell him to either do the blood films now or get one of the nurse or the paediatrician down to do it. If I weren't here, the nurses would have told the paeds to come down fairly quickly anyway. I'm fairly confident that it is viral. The rash she's got is fairly typical and taking bloods now without local anaesthetic while she's so febrile, well, we could end up with her fitting. If she starts convulsing again we'll just go straight in.'

The nurses' station was busy now as the night staff were starting to arrive. Their faces were also made up— even Fay was wearing lipstick—but on the whole they seemed less intimidated by the cameras.

'Evening team.' Samuel smiled. 'All looking particularly lovely tonight—I wonder why.'

Fay grinned. 'It's entirely for your benefit, Samuel, you know that by now.' Sam laughed as Fay continued chatting. 'I couldn't help but notice a huge cheesecake in the fridge.'

'Of course, you had to open the box,' Samuel joked. 'It's a peace offering.'

'Why, what have you done?' Louise asked, as everyone turned to hear.

'Nothing yet,' Samuel said dryly. 'But given the way the night's started, I'm sure I'm going to end up offending one of you lot, so I thought I'd better apologise in advance for my bloody nature and be done with it. Now, Erin and I are going to escape and grab a coffee. Keep an ear out for cot 2,' he added to Fay, referring to Nicola. 'Her temperature's 40.1, and she's still a bit jittery.'

Fay nodded and said, 'Louise, you're down for the paeds area tonight. Why don't you go in there straight away and get the handover from Gemma? I'll fill you in with what's happening everywhere else when I know myself.'

Erin paused. 'I wanted to get the handover filmed,' she said, but Fay shooed her away. 'Go on, you've been here since six. Grab a coffee while you can. I can look after Dave, can't I, darling?' She winked at the cameraman. 'He'll be safe with us.' The nurses let out a few catcalls and Erin was amazed to see Dave actually blushing. With a laugh she gave him a wave and left him to their mercy.

'They're crazy,' she said with a laugh as she followed him into the staffroom. Samuel poured two cups of coffee from a large filter machine.

'Where did that appear from?' Erin asked. 'I've been here all week and I haven't seen it.'

Samuel handed her a cup and she helped herself to a couple of sachets of sugar. 'But you haven't been here at night yet. It's another world. The night staff take their coffee and refreshments very seriously. If you use this machine you have to top it up with water and add another scoop of coffee, or you'll be banned from using it.'

'I'd better remember, then.' She looked over as he sat down and took a sip of his drink. 'Is it always like this?''

'Like what?' he asked.

'So busy. I mean, there's so much going on.'

'I know everyone keeps saying it, but you really haven't seen anything yet. This really isn't busy and I'm not just saying that because you're a reporter. An eighty-year-old with an MI and a baby with a febrile convulsion—as awful as they are for the patient and family—are pretty tame.'

'What will happen to Elsie now?' Erin asked. 'I mean, as far as being admitted.'

'The med. reg. will come and see her, runs some tests and then find her a bed, but as usual we're short of beds so she may be down here a while.'

Erin's brow creased. 'But I spoke with the bed co-ordinator earlier. She told me there were six medical beds empty and one coronary care bed.'

'Which is right, but that doesn't necessarily mean they're the right ones for Mrs White.'

'But she's under Medical—why she would have to wait for a bed when they're up there empty on a ward? For one thing, she'd be more comfortable and surely it would free up a space in Resuscitation for you?' Erin's tone was more questioning than argumentative. She genuinely didn't see what the problem was.

'You're right, but it's not that simple. Look,' Samuel continued as she stared at him with puzzled eyes, 'half the flak we take from patients, relatives and the media is because they simply don't understand the bigger picture. It's one of the reasons I don't want the media here. It's easy to point the camera at the waiting room clock and condemn us because an eighty-year-old, after suffering a heart attack, spends ten hours in Accident and Emergency waiting for a bed while seven beds lie empty on the wards. But the truth is, we saved her life and there's plenty of good reasons why she didn't get moved to one of the beds.'

'So enlighten me,' Erin responded, leaning across the coffee-table. 'Tell me how it really is, and maybe you will be able to make a difference.'

For a moment he stared at her, smoky grey on emerald green. She could see the weight of indecision in the deep pools of his eyes and she held his gaze.

'Tell me,' she repeated steadily.

'Mrs White has had, in layman's terms, a massive heart attack. Now, at the end of the day she's eighty. Sure, we could move her up to one of the medical beds that are vacant and that would be that. She would have her obs done regularly and, no doubt, the nurses would check on her frequently, given that she's had an MI. But you saw for yourself how quickly she collapsed. What if that had happened ten minutes before a nurse came in, or what if the nurse was about to come in but got called away—a phone call perhaps, or someone vomited or wanting a bedpan?'

'So she needs to be monitored more closely. Surely they can put her on a monitor?' Erin protested.

'What good's a monitor if no one's watching it? Like I said, the nurse is on the telephone or another patient's sick, and Elsie is in Room 18 down the end of the ward.'

Erin thought for a moment. 'So why didn't she go to

Coronary Care? Just because she's eighty doesn't mean she doesn't deserve to be treated.'

'Who said anything about not treating her? She's down here on a monitor that's being watched.'

'But there's still an bed empty on Coronary Care,' Erin argued.

Samuel stood up. 'Tell you what, let's resume this conversation at breakfast-time.'

Erin stood up, grumbling. 'But you still haven't explained things.'

Samuel picked up her empty polystyrene cup and, executing a perfect shot, popped it into the bin. 'Breakfast tomorrow,' he said, smiling.

Grudgingly she nodded. 'You've got yourself a date.'

Making her way to the door at the same time as Samuel, they only narrowly avoided a collision.

'Sorry,' they both said at the same time, their eyes catching and holding. For a second they were back in the admin corridor where it had all begun, gently flirting, playing for time to prolong their meeting, and for the craziest moment Erin was utterly positive he was about to kiss her!

CHAPTER FIVE

'SORRY, Sam.' Fay popped her head around the door and Erin hastily dragged her eyes away, blushing crimson. 'I think you might want to take a look at this one, but I'd better put you in the picture first.'

'Fire away.' His voice was as deep and steady as ever and Erin wondered if she'd just imagined the white-hot look that had passed between them.

Fay came and sat on the coffee-table, facing them both, 'You're going to love this one, Erin.' She laughed. 'Deborah Grayson, forty-two years old, eating out tonight at a restaurant—Rolando's, I might add, so she must be loaded.'

'Get to the point,' Samuel said, smiling.

'Sudden onset of severe abdominal cramping.'

'What did she eat?' Samuel asked.

'My question exactly. Antipasto and then calamari for the main course.'

Samuel grimaced. 'So are we expecting the whole restaurant to invade us? Any diarrhoea or vomiting?'

Fay shrugged. 'No to the diarrhoea and just the one vomiting episode, but in my humble opinion she vomited while she was in transition.'

'What?' Samuel said sharply and Erin watched as Fay started to grin broadly.

'It gets better. *Supposedly*, she can't have children and was told so twenty years ago, as they've never used contraception—never thought there was any need.'

Erin was bursting, she simply had to know more.

'You think she's in labour?' she gasped. 'Now?'

Samuel stood up. 'When was her last period?'

'She hasn't had one for ages, in fact, and I quote, "not for about eight or nine months". She assumed it was the change of life. Now, I haven't done midwifery, but I've had a quick feel of her stomach and for the life of me that woman is in second-stage labour. I thought I'd leave you the honour of doing an internal.'

'She's no idea?'

'Not a clue, and half the restaurant are in the waiting room to see if they're about to succumb to food poisoning.'

Erin was practically dancing on the spot. 'Please, let me come with you. Please, Samuel, I just have to see this.' She was beaming.

Fay nodded. 'She's more than happy for the camera to be there—thinks it will help her case when she sues the restaurant.'

'Oh, God,' Samuel muttered. 'Do you reckon she'll make it to the Women's and Children's?'

'No chance,' Fay said happily. 'Put your gloves on, Sam, we're going to have ourselves a delivery.'

As they made their way across the department Samuel turned to Erin. 'If I tell you to get out, go. This woman's obviously had no antenatal care and we don't know if the babe's going to be all right.'

The screams and grunts emitting from cubicle four were practically enough to confirm the diagnosis even without examining the woman.

Dave was happily filming as they entered. Deborah Grayson was standing, leaning against the gurney, but even with the brakes firmly on, Amy, one of the nurses, was struggling to stop it moving as Deborah leaned heavily against it. Louise, at the head of the gurney, was trying to reassure the patient as well as her extremely agitated husband. She gave a wide-eyed look as they entered.

'Hello, I'm Samuel Donovan, the accident and emergency consultant...'

'About time,' Mr Grayson snapped. 'My wife's in agony. Maybe now something can be done.'

Deborah, quieter now, rested her head on her arms. 'Bloody seafood,' she shouted, her affected tones carrying across the department. 'I'll sue the backside off them.' A huge wave of pain engulfed her again and she started to groan.

'Can't you give her something?' Mr Grayson shouted above his wife's moans.

Samuel waited until the pain had abated. 'Mrs Grayson, I'll need to get you up on the trolley so that I can examine you properly.'

Wearily she nodded as Louise and Fay assisted her.

Samuel's examination was deft. Palpating her abdomen skilfully, he kept his hand there. 'Is it coming again?'

'Yes,' she screeched, gasping as the pain yet again overwhelmed her.

'When the pain settles again, I'm going to need to do an internal examination,' Samuel stated.

Without being asked, Dave and Erin stepped outside. ''Struth,' Dave uttered. 'Surely she's guessed what's going on by now. I mean, if I've realised...'

Erin laughed. 'I suppose, if you're not expecting it... Can you just imagine the shock!'

Fay poked her head around the curtain and gave a friendly wink. 'Thanks, guys. You can come back in now.'

'Are you going to give her something?' Mr Grayson demanded.

Samuel shook his head. 'I'm afraid not.' He smiled gently at Mrs Grayson and Erin held her breath as he explained the 'problem' to them both.

'Mrs Grayson, it isn't the seafood you ate that's causing the pain.'

'Of course it is,' Mr Grayson snapped angrily.

Samuel continued. 'The pains you're experiencing, Mrs Grayson, are labour pains.' He paused as the words sank in. 'You're about to deliver a baby.'

'This is ridiculous!' Mr Grayson was ropeable now. 'Come on, Deborah, get dressed. We're going to a private hospital. Come on,' he insisted, grabbing her clothes from under the trolley. 'You lot couldn't diagnose a cold. My wife can't have children—have you any idea the distress your words have caused? You'll be hearing from my lawyer. *Come on*, Deborah.'

'That solicitor sounds like a busy guy,' Fay muttered in an undertone to Erin.

'I think I want to push.' Deborah looked at her husband pleadingly. 'Oh, God, I want to push.'

'It's all right, Deborah.' Samuel spoke kindly, ignoring her husband's angry comments. 'You can push now.'

'But how…?' Mr Grayson asked, his eyes wide. 'I simply don't understand!'

'Hold your wife's hand.' Fay took the bemused man over to the head of the gurney and stayed with them until the contraction had finished.

'I know this is a shock,' Samuel said, 'but we'll deal with the hows and whys later. This baby wants to be born. There isn't time to get you across to the Women's and Children's, but don't worry—you've got a good team on tonight.'

Fay returned with the resuscitation cot and said, 'Paeds are here, seeing the febrile convulsion. They'll be in as soon as they're needed.'

'Are you still happy for the cameras to stay?' Samuel asked the shocked couple. Mr Grayson turned questioningly to his wife and Erin held her breath as she awaited her decision.

'I couldn't care less,' she murmured. 'But can I have an injection?'

'It's too late for that,' Samuel answered. Turning to Fay, he asked, 'Where's the portable Entonox?'

'Being used in the plaster room by the orthopods. They're doing that shoulder reduction.'

So enthralled was Erin by the unfolding events that she momentarily forgot that she was supposed to be a silent observer. 'You could try massaging the small of her back...' As everyone turned to stare, she suddenly remembered her place. 'Sorry,' she said lamely. 'I'll be quiet now.'

And quiet she was, standing there in stunned silence as Mrs Grayson gave in to the urge to push and slowly inched her baby down the birth canal as Samuel coached her. Gasping in wonder as the head emerged, Erin watched intently as Samuel guided Mrs Grayson's hand down so she could feel for herself the hair of her baby. Another push and the rest of the baby followed, its pink slippery body unfolding like petals in the sun as Samuel delivered it and placed it on Deborah's stomach. Overwhelmed and amazed, Deborah reached down for her baby. Fay helped her lift the infant the short distance to its mother's loving arms, the lusty, loud cry of the newborn stilling as it found its mother's breast and instinctively latched on.

Tears were streaming, unchecked, down Erin's and

Louise's cheeks—even Fay was pulling a tissue out of the box.

'Looks like you won't be needing me for a while.' Terence Jenkins, the paediatrician, smiled. 'Everything looks fine. I'll come and have a closer look in a little while. Let Mum and Dad have some time first.'

Samuel nodded. 'Congratulations.' He smiled at the threesome. 'I told you it wasn't the fish.'

Mr Grayson leant over and accepted his handshake. 'Sorry if I came on a bit strong before. I just couldn't believe what I was hearing.' He looked down at his wife and baby. 'If I hadn't seen it for myself...'

Samuel laughed. 'I don't blame you a bit. Once Deborah's delivered the placenta I'll give the Women's and Children's a ring and we can see about getting you all transferred. It will seem a bit more real once you're in a maternity ward and the doctors can help you go over things.'

Deborah tore her eyes away from her baby. 'I can't believe I had a baby inside me and I didn't even know. What are we going to tell everyone?'

Fay, who had wheeled the resuscitation cot back to Resus, reappeared. 'You'd better think of something. I've had a couple of your friends come up and ask for a hot-line number to the Department of Health and Community Services.'

'Oh, no, I forgot they were all here.' Mr Grayson turned to his wife. 'What on earth will I tell them?'

'That when they split the bill for tonight, there's going to be an extra person,' Samuel said dryly.

Mr Grayson grinned. Kissing his wife and child hurriedly, he dashed through the curtains.

'He'll be back in a second,' Samuel said, and sure enough Mr Grayson's face appeared only seconds later.

'Was there something you forgot to ask?' Samuel said, grinning broadly as Mr Grayson walked up to his wife.

'I don't know what we had.'

Deborah looked up from the baby. 'Neither do I,' she said in a dazed voice. 'Neither do I.'

Samuel grinned. 'I was wondering how long it would take. Why don't you both find out?'

With Fay's help Deborah shakingly peeled back the blanket in which her baby was swaddled. 'We've got a daughter, Cedric. It's a little girl.'

Mark was even more ecstatic than Erin had been when she told him.

'We can put it on the news tomorrow. Just a short story to give them a taste, and we'll tell the viewers they can see the whole thing next Sunday night. It will be a ratings winner.'

'You'd better check with them first,' Erin said warily, then grabbed his arm as he headed off toward the cubicles. 'Not now, Mark, for heaven's sake. Tomorrow, at the hospital. Honestly, are ratings all you can think about? That was the most beautiful thing I've ever seen. I just can't get over the fact she didn't even know.'

Mark grinned widely. 'Exactly. It's a great story. All right, I won't go rushing in. I don't want to get Samuel Donovan offside when you've done such a good job of winning him round. Tell you what—I'll send someone over to the Women's and Children's tomorrow, but first thing, mind. I don't want any of the other channels getting wind of this.'

Making her way into the staffroom, Erin was practically bursting to find Fay and Samuel and go over the events. She was somewhat deflated to find them calmly drinking coffee.

'Now, you're not going to tell me that was tame,' she said, plonking herself down on the sofa.

'No,' Samuel agreed. 'That was pretty exciting—for A and E anyway. But it does happen every now and then. Normally, though, it's simply a case that they can't make it the extra five minutes' drive to the Women's and Children's. I've only ever seen it once before where the woman had no idea—how about you, Fay?'

Fay nodded. 'That's right. A couple of years ago, wasn't it, Sam? I was on with you then. Apart from that, only a couple of other times. I'm a bit older than Sam in case you hadn't realised.' She winked. 'So you enjoyed that?' Fay asked, smiling. 'Louise has already decided she wants to apply to be a midwife. How about you, Erin—it didn't put you off having them?'

Erin shook her head. 'It was marvellous, though she did scream pretty loud.'

Samuel shrugged. 'She did very well. That was a big baby and she had no pain control.'

'Massage would have helped, honestly,' she said as Samuel screwed up his nose. 'How about when they realised they didn't know what they'd had?' she said gushingly, but for some reason Fay and Samuel seemed to find her comment hilarious.

'What? What's so funny?' she demanded as they flew into peals of laughter.

Fay tried and failed to stop her giggles, making Samuel only roar louder.

'Tell me!' Erin insisted, and finally they stopped laughing long enough to share the joke.

'It just spoiled the moment...' Fay said breathlessly, wiping away a tear. '"We've got a daughter, *Cedric*. It's a little girl".' And with that they both doubled up again.

'Philistines,' Erin muttered. Turning on her heel, she left them to it.

Erin loved A and E, she loved every moment of it. Her inquisitive nature meant that even the most menial of injuries held a certain fascination for her. It was like a huge kaleidoscope changing with each turn, and no two images were the same.

Watching Samuel Donovan work also held a fascination. No matter how busy, no matter how rushed, he somehow managed to address each patient with courtesy, and listen patiently as they told him the story that explained why they'd ended up there at that particular time. He was also an excellent teacher, authoritatively explaining to Clint his reasons behind his questions and gradually handing over more and more of the reins to him. By the time the waiting room was starting to thin out and some of the patients were at last starting to be moved up to the wards, Clint was working by himself for the most part and running his decisions by Samuel at the nurses' station.

'Right, how are we doing?' Samuel joined Fay as she gazed at the whiteboard.

'Getting there. Elsie White's relatives just arrived and they're not too happy that she's still here.'

Samuel nodded. 'I'll have a word in a moment. How's the febrile convulsion? Clint, what did paeds find?'

Clint looked up from the notes he was writing. 'Probably a viral infection—the lumbar puncture came back clear. They've admitted her, though, as she was still spiking huge temps.'

'No more fits?'

Clint shook his head.

'Good. Where are you up to now?'

Clint gave a small grimace. 'A few left to stitch and then just what's left on the board. For now, anyway.'

'Good man,' Samuel said encouragingly as Clint finished up his notes and headed off to the mini-theatre to start on those awaiting sutures.

'Well, I'll have a word with Elise White's relatives and then I think I might head off to bed.'

Fay nodded. 'Good idea.'

The resuscitation area was quiet, apart from Elsie, and her son and his wife had been allowed to sit with her. Samuel introduced himself.

'Look, we're sorry to make a fuss, but Mum's been down here for seven hours now. The medics said she's waiting for a bed but, from what I can see, patients that came in after her are already being moved to the ward. She's eighty—surely she'd be better in a bed?' Mr White said.

'I understand your concern,' Samuel said sympathetically. 'You're right. Some other medical patients have already been sent up to the ward. The reason your mother is still here is that we need a bed where she can be closely monitored. She'll be wearing a device that uses telemetry, which means that even from a medical ward the nurses on Coronary Care can monitor her heartbeat constantly and if there's any variance they can alert the ward staff promptly. The only problem with that is the equipment has to be at the top end of the ward or the signal simply isn't strong enough. Aside from that, Mrs White really does need a bed near the nurses' station. The other patients haven't been as acutely ill as your mother.'

Mr White nodded, and actually looked relieved. 'Thank you for explaining that to us. I thought it was the other way around, actually. You know, because she's old she was having to wait. But now I understand the reasoning behind it.'

Samuel shook his hand. 'We're keeping a close eye on her here, but hopefully we'll get her up to a ward soon.'

Fay was coming off the telephone as they walked over to the nurses' station. 'The med. reg. just rang. He said to send Mrs White up to the coronary care unit. I've rung them and they're ready for her now.'

'Great. Well, I'm going to crash for a couple of hours. Give me a knock if there's any concerns. How are you finding Clint?' he asked.

Fay gave an enthusiastic nod. 'He's great. He certainly seems to know what he's doing and at least when he's not sure he asks. I think you can rest easy.'

Samuel nodded. 'Yep, I'm pretty impressed with him. Hopefully, the rest of the bunch will be as good. Who knows? We might be in for a good six months.'

Erin found Dave who was filming a young man seemingly the worse for drink, having his hand stitched by Clint. 'How are things going?' she asked the cameraman.

'Great. I thought you were going to have a rest?'

Erin nodded. 'How about you?'

'I'll finish up here and then we might grab a coffee. You go, though. You've got to see out the next fifteen hours or so. At least Phil will be here at seven to relieve me.'

Erin hovered for a moment, watching Clint stitch efficiently away as the patient snored loudly. She knew she really ought to sleep, yet still she was reluctant to leave the hubbub of the department.

Making her way to the on-call room, she met Samuel in the doorway.

'Thanks for tonight. It's been great.'

Samuel nodded. 'It isn't over yet.' For a second their

eyes locked. Erin felt her heart jump into her mouth and she knew at that moment that Anna had been right. Despite her inner and outer protests, Samuel Donovan was a man she would love to get to know better, to somehow break down that harsh exterior and gently explore the man inside. But his words referred only to work, to his beloved department.

'Try and sleep.'

Fat chance there was of that with him in the next room, she thought wildly as she briefly nodded and made her way into the tiny room. Mechanically she washed her face and brushed her teeth and then she lay on the bed, wrestling with the sudden wave of emotions that were overwhelming her. How could she even dare to dream that someone as sophisticated as Samuel could reciprocate her feelings? She was as scatty and disorganised as he was practical and efficient. And yet…he was a passionate man, she just *knew*. The emotive way he expressed himself, the sensual curve of his mouth.

With a groan she rolled over and buried her face in the pillow. She was here to work and nothing else. This was her big break and anyway, she reasoned, he was probably involved with someone—why wouldn't he be? What chance did she have? Resolutely she pushed all thoughts of Samuel Donovan out of her head and willed herself to sleep, but her mind obviously hadn't finished exploring the possibilities because it was Samuel who filled her dreams.

A sharp rap on the door came as an unwelcome intrusion to an extremely pleasant encounter.

'There's a multiple trauma case coming in.' Samuel's voice addressed her with its usual briskness, a sharp contrast to the tender utterances of her dreams. Jumping out of bed, she pulled on her sandals and stepped out of the room, blinking for a second under the harshness of the fluorescent lights.

'What time is it?'

'Four-fifteen. We got a couple of hours in, so we did well.'

Erin followed him to the resuscitation room where the staff were gathered around the empty resuscitation bed, setting up equipment.

His hair was unkempt and his theatre greens were creased but he still managed to look as sexy as the man of her dreams. Jeremy Foster, as immaculate as ever, was vying for a space.

'G'day, Jeremy,' Samuel said dryly. 'I wasn't aware the patient had any abdominal injuries.'

'Neither was I,' said Fay in the same dry tones.

Jeremy wasn't remotely fazed. 'Just thought I'd help out. Save you having to page me.'

The look that Samuel threw at him was completely wasted as Jeremy was looking around anxiously for the camera. Surprisingly, Mark and Dave were nowhere to be seen.

'Have you seen the rest of the team?' Erin asked the gathering staff. The nurses shook their heads but Samuel was less friendly.

'All of my team are here, plus a couple of extras,' he said pointedly, gesturing to Jeremy. 'They're busy enough without keeping tabs on your mob.'

Erin rolled her eyes. 'I only asked.' After a brief look around the department she still couldn't locate them but as the overhead system piped up, asking the trauma team to come to the emergency department, Erin relaxed. Wherever they were, they'd surely hear that.

They obviously did as, somewhat ruffled, they arrived

just ahead of the patient who was wheeled in, groaning loudly.

'Car versus tree,' the paramedic announced as he and his partner raised the trolley to the height of the resuscitation bed.

'Name is Mr Waterman. Conscious on arrival, it took an hour to free him. His left leg was trapped—open fracture dislocation.' He carried on reciting the injuries to the patient as they lifted him onto the bed, with Samuel holding the patient's head and neck.

'Where have you been?' Erin asked. Mark pointedly didn't reply and Dave was too busy filming.

'Where were you?' she repeated, and Mark finally responded.

'We just followed one of the admissions up to the ward,' he said casually, but he couldn't quite meet her eyes and Erin was convinced there was something he wasn't telling her. There was no time to interrogate him further, though, as the next half-hour was spent watching the flurry of activity around the patient.

The paramedics had advised that the patient's breath had smelt strongly of alcohol and Erin felt a growing anger burn inside her as she listened to Mr Waterman slurring his words as he shouted expletives at the staff who were trying to help him.

To Jeremy's utter frustration, the patient's abdomen seemed to have escaped any injury and, in fact, once cleaned up and assessed, it appeared that apart from a serious leg fracture and a multitude of small lacerations and bruises he had got off relatively lightly. Most of the staff dispersed as the patient was wheeled around for his X-rays with a nurse escort. Erin listened as Samuel discussed his injuries with the orthopaedics.

'Bloody lucky, if you ask me. Apparently the car's a

write-off and the tree's totally down. He's got so much alcohol on board I'm amazed he thought to put his seat belt on. It's the only thing that saved him. His leg's a mess, though.'

The orthopaedic registrar grabbed the films out of the trolley as the patient was wheeled past. 'I'll be with you in a moment, Mr Waterman. I just want to see your X-rays.'

Mr Waterman nodded, quieter now but obviously in great discomfort.

Erin watched quietly as Amy checked his blood pressure and did his observations, swapping his oxygen mask for nasal cannulas.

'Are you sure there's no one you want me to ring for you?' Amy asked, but Mr Waterman didn't respond to her question. 'You'll be going up to Theatre shortly. There must be someone you want informed—you've been in a nasty accident after all.'

Finally he nodded. 'I'd besht let the wife know. She won't come, though. The kids will be ashleep.'

The same anger she had felt on Mr Waterman's arrival resurfaced as Erin listened to his slurring words. This man had caused so much pain, not only to himself but also to his wife and children, all because he had drunk too much and decided to drive. Her heart went out to Mrs Waterman, picking up the phone at this hour of the morning and being given the bad news.

'My wallet.' He gestured to the bag of clothes which had been temporarily thrown into the corner. 'Could you pass my bag?' He looked over to Erin and she looked away quickly. 'Hey, you, can youse pass up me bag?'

Erin bristled at his tone. She had no sympathy for this man, none. The only good thing he had done that night had been to hit a tree and not another car. For a second her mind flashed back to ten years ago. Her father's yell of horror alerting them, looking up as an oncoming car weaved its way towards them, the screech of brakes as her father fought to save his family. And then the deafening noises of the impact—the screams, the breaking glass—followed by an eerie silence.

Erin closed her eyes. She could still picture the drunk that had slaughtered her parents being loaded into the ambulance, oblivious to what he had done. The hatred she'd felt as she'd stood at the roadside wrapped in a blanket, being comforted by a policewoman, was as vivid now as it had been then.

'Hey, lady, passh me bag.'

Erin swung her face around, her eyes blazing. 'I'm here to observe only.' That was all she said, but the utter contempt in her voice was so apparent that Fay, Amy and Samuel looked over questioningly.

'I'll get it,' Fay said quickly, retrieving the bag and helping with the search for his wallet.

'What was that all about?' Samuel strode over and hissed darkly into her ear.

'Nothing,' Erin said defiantly. 'I'm here to observe only—I thought that was what you wanted?'

Samuel shook his head, his eyes blazing. 'You were all set to give Mrs Grayson a bloody massage, you cried your eyes out about Elise White. So what's the deal here, Erin?'

Erin returned his angry stare, her small face rigid. 'He could have wiped out a whole family. He doesn't deserve my sympathy. He's a drunk.' The malice in her voice surprised even Erin, but it was as if all her anger from long ago was somehow channelled into this moment. Samuel stared at her for a second, his face bewildered, and then his anger returned.

'He's a patient, *my* patient, and don't you ever forget it. Now get the hell out of this resuscitation room, and if I see you anywhere near Mr Waterman again I'll have the whole lot of you thrown out. Go on, get out.' His tone was still deathly quiet but there was no mistaking the fury behind his words. Smartly, proudly, Erin turned on her heel and left the area. Mark came rushing up.

'Why aren't you in there?' he demanded.

'Apparently I wasn't being nice enough to Mr Donovan's patients. He asked me to leave.' Her voice was shaky and she could feel the tears pricking at her eyes.

'Dave's still in there, though?' Mark questioned, and Erin nodded. Mark couldn't care less how Erin was feeling as long as the show went on.

'I'll go in there with him. It's all pretty quiet out here. Maybe you should go back to bed for a bit, give him a chance to calm down. He's a moody one all right, that Samuel Donovan. Don't worry about it.'

But she wasn't going to escape Samuel's wrath so easily. Outside the on-call room he caught up with her.

'What on earth was all that about?' He ran a hand through his tousled hair and searched her face questioningly, the anger still in his voice.

'I just saw red,' Erin admitted. 'I mean, he's so drunk he can hardly speak, and when he said, "Hey lady"... I don't appreciate being spoken to like that.' She remained defiant but she knew she was losing.

Samuel shook his head angrily. 'So the patients are supposed to cater to your feminist ideal, are they? How did you want to him to address you, Erin?'

She didn't answer but Samuel carried on. '*Ms* Casey perhaps. Would that have been better? My God, you're such a hypocrite.'

That got her, and Erin found her tongue. 'I'm not,' she replied furiously.

'Yes, you are,' he hissed. 'A big one. You make out you're so unmaterialistic, such a man of the people, or should I say person of the people? It's easy to say money doesn't matter when you've got some. It's all very easy to spout off about your social ideals, to sponsor a couple of kids and not eat meat, and you think you're doing your bit for mankind. But when push comes to shove you're every bit the middle-class madam you so vehemently oppose.'

'I'm not,' she retorted, furious now. 'At least I try to make a difference. I know all I can do is a small bit—we can't all go home knowing we saved a life today. But I do try where I can.' She was struggling not to cry now. 'Why do you always have to ridicule me? We can't all be like you, *Doctor*.'

But Samuel was unmoved by her response. 'Try?' He said incredulously. 'You really think you try? Well, let me tell you this much—you only try when it suits you, when it's the politically correct thing to do. When it comes to the real world and real problems, you're not so charitable then, are you?'

'Yes, I am,' she argued. 'He's brought his problems on himself. If he hadn't been drinking—'

Samuel cut her short. 'Two weeks ago that man had a nice life. Middle-level management, a wife and a couple of kids. Then he lost his job. He's spent the last fortnight having doors slammed in his face. Last night his wife tells him she's leaving and taking the kids. Apparently she didn't fancy being married to a loser. So Mr Waterman does what a lot of people would do in the circumstances, and drowned his sorrows. His big mistake was deciding to drive over to where his wife was staying and trying to reason with her.'

Erin listened, horrified, as Samuel continued his story.

'Not only has he lost his job, wife and kids, but by the time he returns from Theatre he'll probably have lost his leg as well and, no doubt, his driver's licence to boot. All that guy's got to look forward to is months of rehab and a drunk-driving court case, plus a messy divorce. The last thing he needs is some jumped up journo looking down her nose at him.

'This is an accident and emergency department. There's no dress code here. No list on the door, stating the required attributes needed to be seen. Everyone deserves to be treated, and if you can't stretch to compassion for someone down on their luck, then at least show a little respect for a fellow human being.'

There was nothing Erin could say. It took a superhuman effort to simply nod as she struggled to hold back her tears. The contempt in Samuel's eyes, the anger in his voice had all been directed at her this time and, what's more, Erin acknowledged, she'd deserved it.

CHAPTER SIX

How long she lay there, gazing into the darkness, Erin never knew. She was half reeling from Samuel's damning words and half stunned at her outburst towards an unknown human being for, despite what Samuel had inferred, she truly did care about others. But it wasn't only that she dealt with as she lay there on the bed. Suddenly all the pain of yesteryear seemed to have surfaced—the buried grief at losing her parents, the senseless waste of life, the aching, empty void that could never, ever be filled. But she didn't cry. It was almost as if tears would have been a paltry offering for the pain she felt.

A soft knocking at the door was left unacknowledged, and when Samuel flicked on the nightlight and sat on the bed beside her, she didn't even blink.

'It was a drunk driver that killed your parents, wasn't it?' He was still for a moment before he continued. 'I couldn't remember all the details. Fay just reminded me.'

'Fay remembered as well?'

'I spoke to her about it on Thursday after you'd gone. She knew she recognised you but couldn't quite put her finger on where from.' He paused for a long moment before continuing. 'Erin, we might seem hardened and clinical but it affects us all. What happened to you and Anna was a tragedy. Everyone who was on that day would have taken a bit of it home with them. I'm not in any way comparing it to the pain you feel, just trying to let you know we understand the magnitude of your loss.'

Her voice was monotone, shallow. 'It was a long time ago.'

'Doesn't matter,' he said resolutely. 'It must be agony.'

His acknowledgement of her pain and the insight of his words brought the heavily resisted tears forth, and with an angry sob she wiped furiously at her face.

'That poor man.' Her words were strangled by her tears. 'Should I apologise?''

A tiny smile tugged at the corner of his mouth. 'Erin, you did nothing wrong. I overreacted.'

Erin shook her head. 'Yes, I did. You heard the way I spoke to him.'

'Mr Waterman is completely wasted. He doesn't even know what year it is—not that that's an excuse not to treat him with dignity, of course. Look, Erin, you *were* out of line but in all honesty you really weren't that bad. I overreacted, don't ask me why. Like you, I just saw red.'

He pulled a couple of tissues from the box by her bedside. Instead of offering them to her, he gently wiped away the tears from her cheeks. Erin was stunned and touched at this sudden display of affection. Through her tears she somehow focused on his haughty features, softened in the nightlight's glow, and in his eyes Erin knew for sure that she could see more than just compassion.

There was something about raw emotion that made small talk superfluous. At that moment Erin inwardly acknowledged the depth of her feeling towards him. Her voice was trembling, soft, but the question was direct. 'Don't ask you why because you don't know, or because you're not telling?'

He turned his face and stared at her. 'Both,' came his husky reply. She gazed back at him for the longest moment. She so badly wanted him to take her in his arms for him to kiss away the pain and the hurt, to impulsively act upon the attraction she knew they both felt. But, of course, it didn't happen. Instead, he stood up. Turning off the light, he quietly left the room and Erin lay there, her mind filled with a load of new questions.

Her body was tired now, her legs ached and her eyes were sore, but her mind was too alert for sleep. Making her way out of the on-call room, she walked slowly around the department. Mark had finally gone home to bed but Dave walked around with her, filming as they went. The department was in chaos, as if some wild party had been held there. A couple of nurses were lethargically restocking the dressing trolleys while the others tended to the few patients remaining. Samuel and Clint were both in the two unit theatres, suturing the last few patients. A couple of drunks were sleeping in the waiting room, in no rush to be seen.

Louise made her way over to the whiteboard where Fay was making a few alterations.

'I'm just going to take cot 1 up to the children's wards.'

Fay nodded. 'What did the paed say?'

'Bronchiolitis and mild dehydration. She's struggling to feed. The paediatrician is going to put an IV in up on the ward.'

Fay shook her head. 'Is the paeds resident down here still?'

'He's just finishing up his notes.'

'Well, tell him to get IV access down here. That baby's not well and you know how quickly they can go off. Mild dehydration can become moderate to marked very quickly.' Fay smiled at Erin who was watching quietly.

'Down here we've always got a doctor. As much as the paediatrician might intend to go to the ward and start an infusion, anything can happen which might delay him. At least if he puts a bung in down here and writes up some IV orders, the nurses on the ward can relax a bit.'

Erin listened intently. Fay was so knowledgeable yet she imparted it so effortlessly. She really was a marvellous teacher.

'It's a huge responsibility, being in charge of such a busy unit. How do you deal with it?'

Fay shrugged. 'Cheesecake helps.' She laughed and took a mouthful of the cake Samuel had bought in.

'But surely it must take its toll on you? Do you find yourself worrying about patients once you get home or are you able to switch off and leave it all behind?'

Fay gave a self-conscious look at the camera and then started to laugh. 'I'm sorry, Erin, I can't stop.'

'Fay, please,' Erin protested. 'I'm supposed to get some interviews.'

'I don't mind you following me about and that, but as soon as you point that thing at me and put on your serious voice...' She started to laugh again.

Louise, once she returned from the ward, was equally as useless in front of the camera. Far from laughing self-consciously, Louise loved the camera, flicking her hair back, licking her lips seductively and dropping her voice to answer Erin's questions.

This time it was Erin who ended up laughing. 'Louise, we just want you to be natural. It's an in-depth report we're doing, not soft porn.'

'You'll get nothing out of this lot at this time of the morning.' Even before Samuel spoke, Erin was aware of his presence. 'Fay, we're practically up to date with the stitching. I've left a couple for Clint to do.' He sniffed the air. 'Can you smell that bacon? The canteen must be firing up their ovens. I might go and get some breakfast.'

'And a strong coffee.'

Samuel nodded. 'It's going to be a busy hand clinic this morning and from the amount of X-rays on the desk a busy plaster clinic, too.'

'You'd better take Erin for a strong coffee, too,' Fay said, noticing Erin yawn.

Samuel didn't say anything, but he gestured for Erin to follow him.

'I just have to get my purse,' she muttered, suddenly as self-conscious as Fay and Louise had been.

'I'm sure I can stretch to a bacon butty,' Samuel said irritably, but Erin was adamant.

'Absolutely not. I always pay my own way. And anyway, I'm a vegetarian.'

Samuel rolled his eyes. 'Women's lib's got a lot to answer for,' he muttered as he followed her to her room. 'By the time we get there I'll be paged to come back.' Instead of waiting politely outside this time, he followed her into the room.

'My God,' he said as he looked around. 'All you need is a cat sitting on the floor! Do you want me to pinch a few flowers from the ward to make it just a bit more homely?'

Erin gave a tight smile. 'It's only a few books and toiletries,' she said as Samuel looked around, open-mouthed.

'Well, I hope they don't send you to the desert for your next assignment if this is what you need for one night away. Imagine the supplies you'd take if you were away for a couple of weeks—they'd need an extra camel to lug this lot.'

Retrieving her purse, they headed off to the canteen, stopping at the kiosk on the way to buy the Sunday papers. Erin immediately opened the colour supplement and turned to the back page, reading the horoscope for Taurus as they walked along. Hopefully, Louis Sapphire was right, she thought with a smug smile as she read about her week ahead.

'So what's in store for me, then?'

Erin gave him a suspicious look. 'Don't pretend you believe in it. You don't have to humour me.'

'I'm not. Come on, read me the horoscope for Taurus.'

'You're a Taurus, too?' Erin blinked.

'Why, don't I act like one?'

Erin looked him up and down. Earthy, passionate, sensual—that just about summed him up really. Instead, she answered somewhat sarcastically, 'Well, you look like a maddened bull when you're talking to the med. reg. so, yes, I guess you do.'

'So come on, then, read me our stars.'

Erin couldn't help but blush as she stammered out the prediction.

'''Some things are meant to be. So instead of resisting why not just give in and let the fabulous journey the stars have in store for you evolve. Even you deserve a little romance and spoiling. Pay extra attention to anything official in the post.'''

'Well, that safely covers half the population. I'll be sure to read my bank statement with renewed interest.'

'Louis Sapphire is very accurate,' Erin said defensively.

'And very rich, no doubt,' Samuel replied dryly.

They bagged a table on the decking outside the canteen and Erin picked at a bowl of muesli while Samuel tucked unashamedly into a huge mountain of bacon toasties.

'Sure you don't want one?' he offered, pushing the plate over to her. Erin shook her head primly. 'They'd be a lot tastier than that horse food you live on.'

'At least this "horse food" isn't clogging up my coronary arteries,' she retorted.

Samuel gave her a knowing look. 'Go on, you know you want one really.'

'Speaking of coronary arteries,' Erin said brightly as Samuel groaned into his coffee, 'you never did explain to me why Elsie wasn't given the coronary care bed.'

'She was. It just took a while for her to get there.'

Catching her eye over the rim of his coffee-cup, Samuel gave a long sigh. 'I'm not going to get off that easily, am I?' He replaced his cup in the saucer. 'All right, what is it you want to know?'

'Why she waited so long when the bed was there all the time? You saw her relatives were getting upset, you knew the cameras were in the department and you knew there was an empty bed. Yet you still kept her waiting for over seven hours. It just seems like bad PR.'

Samuel yawned and stretched lazily in his chair before answering. 'All right, then, try and picture this, *Ms* Casey. You're married, five years or so now, a couple of kids, another on the way.'

Erin flushed. 'What's that got to do with it?'

'Now, just imagine for a moment that Mr Casey has a heart attack. He's been under a lot of pressure, working hard to keep you in crystals and essential oils.'

Erin fought a sudden urge to kick Samuel under the table. 'My husband would be far too relaxed and laid-back to suffer from stress. I'd burn some frankincense or lavender oil, give him a long massage—that would soothe him.'

'It's probably what finished him off in the first place. All right, he's been battling with his cholesterol, but apart from that—'

'No way,' Erin interrupted. 'My husband wouldn't be slavering over bacon butties and the like.'

Samuel grinned. 'He sounds as boring as hell. Are you going to let me finish?'

Erin nodded.

'Well, for whatever reasons, your husband has suffered a major heart attack. Now, how would you feel if you were told that all the coronary care beds were full?'

Erin shrugged. 'Disappointed, I guess, but that's the way the health system is. You can't keep a permanent bed empty in case *my* husband has a heart attack.'

'Good answer,' Samuel said encouragingly. 'And one I've used to the board when we've discussed the same. Now, and I want you to be honest here, suppose you found out that Coronary Care was full of eighty- and ninety-year-olds?'

Erin's brow furrowed, then she answered defiantly, 'I'd just have to swallow it. You said yourself that everyone deserves treatment. Just because someone's old...' Her voice trailed off as she pondered the scenario.

'Tough call, isn't it?' His voice broke into her thoughts.

'But Elsie still got the coronary care bed. What if a young patient had come in after she'd been sent up?'

Samuel drained his coffee before he replied. 'As you pointed out, we can't keep a bed indefinitely. Look, it's all a big juggling game. Had someone come in after two a.m., by the time they'd been seen and sorted there would have been a bed on Coronary Care for them. We could give them their initial treatment in A and E, and Coronary Care would do a bed shuffle in the morning, after which the A and E patient could go up with no harm done and only six or seven hours in A and E. That's probably why the med. reg. was holding off from giving the bed to Elsie. He's got a lot of responsibility on his shoulders. That could, realistically speaking, have been the last coronary care bed in the whole of the city, so it makes it a pretty precious commodity.

'Look, Erin,' he added passionately, 'you can report this either way. You can make us look like sinners or saints but the truth is that no one, and I mean no one, likes playing God. No one likes having to share out the slices of the apple where lives are concerned. But tough decisions have to made every hour of every day in this hospital, probably every minute, and all we can do is try to do our best with what's available. Now, that's enough talk about work.' He gave her a wicked grin. 'Go on, have a bacon sandwich. They're going fast.'

Erin chose to ignore him, pretending to concentrate instead on the accommodation section of the newspaper as she mulled over what he'd just said. Samuel was right, she admitted grudgingly to herself. That bacon *did* smell marvellous. Giving up meat had been a conscious decision she'd made years ago and one she'd found relatively easy, but there was something about the smell of bacon…

'What are you reading?' Samuel interrupted her thoughts.

'The paper,' she answered, without looking up.

'I can see that. Why are you looking at the rentals?'

With a sigh Erin put down her paper and looked over the table at him. She still felt embarrassed about her behaviour last night and extremely awkward, being alone with him, but from the way Samuel was casually chatting he obviously wasn't aware of the effect he had on her.

'I'm going to be taking in a lodger. I was just looking to see how much rent they paid, except I can't see any in the Camberwell area. There can't too many properties for rent at the moment.'

'You've looked into this properly, I take it.'

'Of course,' Erin lied.

'The major rental section is in *Saturday's* newspaper, Erin. I think you might find what you're looking for there. Tell you what.' He relented as he saw how uncomfortable he'd made her. 'I've got a copy in the car. I'll go and get it for you later.' Samuel looked at her consideringly for a moment. 'What are you going to write? ''Crystal-loving vegetarian, into massage and aromatherapy, seeks housemate''? You'd better be careful—heaven knows what lunatics you might attract.'

Erin put down her coffee-cup. 'So I'm a lunatic now, am I, as well as a hypocrite?'

Samuel grinned at her outburst. 'Not at all. I just think you should think carefully before you place an ad and open up your home to strangers. Anyway, why do you need to take in a lodger?'

She hesitated before telling him, but once she'd started Erin amazed herself as she opened up. Samuel listened intently.

'I have to agree with your sister,' he said finally when she'd finished explaining. 'It really is a huge commitment.'

'But I can't sell the home—you wouldn't understand,' she said.

Samuel leant back in his chair and eyed her thoughtfully for a moment. 'Actually, I understand far more than you realise. My father died a few years ago, and my mother is in extremely poor health. She's in a nursing home.'

Erin looked up at him. 'I'm sorry.'

'The house was sitting empty, I couldn't bear to sell it, but it was either that or see it end up falling into disrepair or, worse, getting burgled. It was hard, though, I admit that.'

Erin nodded. 'Why didn't you move in?'

He considered her question for a moment before answering, 'Because as much as you don't want to admit it, eventually you come to realise that things can never be the same again, and keeping the dream alive by not selling only prolongs the agony.'

His words made sense, she knew that, but she just wasn't ready to hear them. Hastily she changed the subject. 'It must be hard, working those long hours. It must put a huge strain on your relationships.' She flushed as the words tumbled out. She had only meant to change the subject, not interrogate him about his personal life! Still, she was simply dying to hear the answer. But Samuel answered evenly, apparently not remotely bothered by her question.

'I don't have time for relationships.'

'Surely not,' Erin argued. 'Are you trying to tell me that anyone considering a career in Accident and Emergency snaps on a chastity belt?'

'I don't think a chastity belt would be appropriate for my anatomy,' he said, laughing as Erin blushed before he continued. 'Look, of course not. Most of my colleagues are happily married. It's probably the one thing that keeps them sane. It's just not for me.'

'So you've never had a relationship?' Erin asked incredulously.

'Of course I have,' he admitted, and Erin saw his face darken. 'I was even married for a while there, but it didn't work out.'

'Why?' she asked nosily.

'This is off the record I assume?'

Erin nodded eagerly, leaning over the table to catch his words.

'It's none of your business,' he said, laughing at her obvious irritation.

Erin sat back in her chair, but a terrible thought suddenly occurred to her. 'You're not gay, are you?'

'And you're not backward at coming forward! No, I'm not gay. Where did you pluck that from?'

Erin managed to look sheepish. 'Just the way you're being so cagey.'

'Erin, you're a reporter, for heaven's sake. It hardly makes for a relaxing breakfast chat. And what would it matter if I were gay? For someone who professes to be so liberally minded, you do seem rather conservative at times.'

Erin didn't know how to respond. If the truth were told, she couldn't have cared less if the whole of the accident and emergency unit were the front float at the Sydney Mardi Gras, so long as it didn't involve Samuel. Oh, she knew he was miles out of her league, but to have been so completely and utterly out of the equation just wouldn't have been fair.

Samuel leant across the table, his eyes looking into hers as he spoke. Erin was mesmerised. 'All right, I'll word it better. I'm not husband material. You've sworn yourself off meat, I've sworn myself off marriage. Sure, it might be tempting sometimes.' He glanced at the remnants of his breakfast before returning his eyes to hers. 'As you know all too well. But sometimes you just have to look at the bigger picture and stand by your commitments.'

'You can't compare marriage to a bacon sandwich,' Erin argued, but his pager interrupted her protests.

'Saved by the bell,' Samuel said, standing up. 'Now, let's get back to it.'

As she followed him along the narrow corridor her mind was whirring. Why would someone as gorgeous and sensual as Samuel Donovan vow himself off relationships? She knew it was a pipe dream to consider that he would even look twice at herself, but he must have heaps of offers. To rule marriage out entirely, to be so resolute that it wasn't for him—what on earth had made him like that? She thought about how his face had darkened when he'd spoken of his marriage. His ex-wife must have hurt him badly. She looked at his broad shoulders, his long athletic stride and for a moment she shook her head in wonder. Whoever she was, she must have been crazy. How, Erin tried to fathom, could you not want that?

CHAPTER SEVEN

BY THE time they got back to the unit the staff had changed over and yet again the waiting room was starting to fill up with patients, though most were waiting to be seen in either the hand or plaster clinic. Samuel, Erin knew, had only slept for two or maybe three hours, yet still he managed to remain attentive and polite to all the patients.

Several were hungover and obviously feeling somewhat sheepish. Others were determined to voice their anger over the wait they'd endured the previous day. Each patient was examined carefully and listened to, Samuel addressing them in compassionate yet authoritative tones. His PR work was excellent and Erin saw that most if not all of the patients left the department feeling their visit had been worthwhile.

The day seemed to whiz by. The pace wasn't as frantic as on weekdays, Erin was informed, but the gurneys quickly filled with various patients wearing their footy jumpers and clutching their ankles, along with the usual cuts and falls. Jeremy finally had his moment in the sun with a couple of patients with abdominal pains and the chest medical doctors were kept busy with an apparent sharp raise in asthmatics—a byproduct of the hot, humid weather Melbourne was experiencing.

'It's worse in Sydney. The weather's very humid there,' Vicki explained as she tapped away at the computer. 'I worked there for a couple of years. This child isn't too bad, but she'll need to go straight through and have some obs done and get a nebuliser.'

Erin nodded. 'My sister has bad asthma. She uses the sprays but when it's really bad she goes onto a nebuliser. We've been up here a few times with her.'

Vicki didn't answer as an elderly couple came up to the desk, sliding their admission form under the security glass. Vicki read the paperwork briefly as she introduced Erin and explained what she was there for.

'Now, Mr Reed,' Vicki said to the pale-looking man, 'I'm Sister Vicki Lynbrook, the triage nurse today. It says here that you've got back pain.'

Mr Reed nodded and opened his mouth to answer, but his wife interrupted impatiently.

'I told him he shouldn't be fiddling up the ladder at his age. Silly old beggar. No wonder he's hurt his back.'

'It's got nothing to do with being up the ladder,' Mr Reed answered irritably. 'That was yesterday I was up the ladder. This just came on this morning.'

'Well, happen you strained yourself.'

Erin smiled to herself as she listened to the argumentative couple, and waited for Vicki to type in a three or possibly a four, but Vicki hadn't finished her questions yet.

'Did you fall or strain yourself?'

Mr Reed shook his head.

'Do you suffer with a bad back?'

Again he shook his head. Suddenly he gripped the desk tightly, beads of sweat forming on his brow.

In a flash Vicki had pressed a button by the desk. Pushing the green exit button, she made her way around and guided the patient to a chair.

'Sorry,' he said somewhat breathlessly. 'I just came over all dizzy. I'm fine now.'

Vicki carried on questioning him as a nurse appeared with a gurney. 'Have you got pain anywhere else?'

His hand motioned towards his stomach and he nodded feebly.

'You never said that to me,' his wife remarked loudly.

Mr Reed rolled his eyes. 'You never gave me a chance.'

'We're just going to get you up onto the gurney.' Gently the two nurses assisted him, and Erin was alarmed when she heard Vicki speak in low tones to the other nurse.

'Get him straight through, Jenny, and tell Sam to have a look at him. It could be a triple A.' Vicki turned to Erin and said, 'You might want to watch this one.'

The nurse was struggling with the trolley. 'Can you help me push?' she asked. Erin nodded and took hold of the trolley, helping to push it through the heavy black swing doors.

'What's the story?' Samuel asked, coming straight over.

Briefly he introduced himself to Mr Reed as he listened to Jenny's report.

'Vicki said he was a back pain and to get him seen straight away. That's all I know.'

'He said he had stomach pain as well,' Erin ventured, then stopped herself. But instead of appearing annoyed at her interruption, Samuel actually gave her an appreciative nod.

'Mr Reed, I'm just going to have feel your stomach.' Jenny was hovering and it was practically left to Samuel to undress the patient as she rummaged under the trolley to find a gown.

'We might just pop some oxygen on. What's his BP?'

he asked the young nurse, who was now struggling with the automatic cuff.

Samuel reached over impatiently. 'You have to turn it on first,' he said curtly as he slipped a green oxygen mask over Mr Reed's face.

'Mr Reed, I'm just giving you some oxygen through this mask. I know you're in a lot of pain and as soon as we know what's going on we'll give you something to help.' He stopped just long enough to place a reassuring hand on Mr Reed's shoulder and give it a gentle squeeze. 'You hang in there, mate. We'll look after you.'

The fear that was blatant in Mr Reed's eyes abated somewhat as he nodded back at Samuel. Erin was stunned. This was a man who, ten minutes ago, had walked into the department. Had it been up to Erin, he would have been politely told to go and sit in the waiting room. But to look at him now, lying flat on the hospital gurney and as pale as the hospital gown he was wearing, it was blatantly obvious, even to Erin's untrained eye, that this man was desperately ill.

'Let's get some IV access. He needs a couple of large-bore cannulae, and page the surgeons.' Samuel's instructions were clear and concise but Jenny, for whatever reason, didn't seem to realise the urgency of the situation and went to leave the area.

'Not you,' Samuel said. His voice was calm but Erin could see the frustration in his eyes at the nurse's obvious lack of experience and realisation of the urgency of the situation. 'Press the bell and get someone else to do it, and get some help in here.'

A familiar face appeared around the curtains. 'Everything all right?'

Samuel didn't waste time asking Fay why she was here

so early, and Erin saw the look of urgency that passed between them.

In an instant she took over. 'Mr Reed, when Mr Donovan has finished putting the IV in and taking your blood, I'm going to move you into another area where there's a bit more room.'

Samuel questioned Mr Reed gently as he took the blood. When he was finished, Fay, in one deft movement, kicked the brake off the gurney and then connected the oxygen tubing from the wall supply to the portable cylinder under the gurney. 'Jenny, take Mrs Reed into interview room one and tell her someone will be with her shortly.'

Undoubtedly there was something serious going on, but neither Samuel nor Fay betrayed anything other than a quiet air of efficiency.

By the time a hasty set of portable X-rays had been taken, Jeremy Foster had appeared with his resident. For the first time he didn't seem remotely conscious of the cameras as he made his way straight over to the patient's bedside. In a sharp contrast to Samuel's platitudes and gentle explanations, Jeremy didn't even bother to introduce himself before examining the patient's abdomen. Not that Mr Reed was well enough to notice. The deterioration in his condition was alarming. Jeremy nodded to Samuel as he felt for Mr Reed's femoral pulses.

'Do you want an ultrasound?' Samuel asked. 'They're ready for you.'

Jeremy shook his head. 'I think we'd better just get him straight up. Can someone let Theatre know?'

'I've told them. They're getting ready. I've done all the blood work and he's had some X-rays. He just needs the consent signed.'

Jeremy nodded impatiently. 'See to it, Shona,' he said curtly to his resident. 'I'll go on and scrub.'

'Jeremy.' Samuel's single word was enough to stop Jeremy in his tracks as he started to make a hasty departure to Theatre. Samuel handed him the consent form.

'Mr Reed came in with a back pain. You need to explain this to him properly. I'll talk to his wife.'

Jeremy turned and made his way over to the patient. Erin watched as he coughed and cleared his throat. With a start she realised he was nervous.

'Mr Reed, you have what we call a dissecting abdominal aortic aneurysm. The aorta is the main artery in your body, and it's leaking.' He drew a very rough diagram on the back of the consent form. 'I know this must be a huge shock, but we have to get you up to Theatre quickly. It's like a balloon that could burst. We have to repair it *now*.' His words didn't come as easily as Samuel's, but despite his initial reluctance he did speak kindly to the patient, going into slightly greater detail and warning Mr Reed of the risks involved. To Erin it seemed cruel, telling someone there was a very real chance they might die, but she knew enough to know that the consent had to be informed. 'It's a very serious operation, I have to tell you that,' Jeremy warned him.

Mr Reed managed a small nod.

'Do you understand what I've told you?' he asked, and again Mr Reed nodded.

Jeremy gave him a smile. 'I'm good at this, Mr Reed,' he almost whispered, and as his back was now to the camera, Erin knew his smile and cocky but comforting words were meant solely for the patient.

'I need you to sign this consent form. Do you have any questions?'

Mr Reed struggled to lift his hand and managed only

a scrawl. Lifting his hand, he tried to remove the mask but he was too weak and it was Jeremy who removed the oxygen mask for him to enable him to hear.

'My wife...'

'She's here.' Samuel appeared in the doorway with a very subdued Mrs Reed. 'You go on up, Jeremy. Thanks.'

Erin could hardly bear to watch as Mrs Reed made her way over to the gurney and gave her husband a cuddle. Everyone stood back and allowed the couple as much as they could to have a moment's privacy. Erin felt her eyes fill up. What would she say to him? she wondered. How do you sum up a life together in a few seconds?

It was Samuel who stepped in. 'We really have to get him up now.'

Mrs Reed nodded, her face contorted with fear as she watched the man she loved being wheeled away.

And then he was gone. Erin watched as Fay guided Mrs Reed to the interview room, and for once Erin had no desire to follow.

She watched as the staff cleared away the mess, checking and replacing the equipment carefully, getting ready for the next unlucky person who would need their services, the next unfortunate individual whose life would change at the roll of the dice. 'Keep filming,' she muttered to Phil, who had replaced Dave behind the camera. 'I want to get all this.'

Fay walked up to her. 'That,' she said, 'was the biggest surgical emergency you'll see. Response time is all-important, and we did well to get him up to Theatre so quickly.'

'I just didn't realise how sick he was.'

'Neither did the nurse looking after him,' Fay said astutely. 'Jenny's new, thinks she knows everything and doesn't like to be told anything. The truth is, she's got a lot to learn. I'll be having a few words with her soon—but, anyway, that's my problem. How has it been today?'

Erin managed a smile. 'Interesting. How long will he be in Theatre for?'

'A few hours. No news is good news—for a while at least. If he makes it he should be out by the time you finish up.'

'What are you doing here? I thought you weren't on until tonight,' Erin queried.

'I'm not but someone has to sort out the roster—we're way down for next week. I was hoping to pop in and grab it and pop straight out again.'

'You must love what you do, though?' Erin probed.

'It's all right. Phil's filming the clearing-up, not us.'

'I love nursing but I have to admit I'm not too keen on being the unit manager. Still, someone has to do it.'

'But I would have thought there would have been heaps of people after that job. If you don't like it, why do you do it?'

Fay looked at her consideringly for a moment. 'We used to have a great unit manager here. She was very young, but brilliant. Ran the place like clockwork. She had to leave suddenly due to personal reasons.' Fay lowered her voice. 'Namely Jeremy Foster. But that's another story. And you're right—there were lots of applicants for her position but no one was really suitable. I'm not blowing my own trumpet but it takes a hell of a lot more than a uni degree and a critical care course to run a place like this. A few of the staff that applied will, no doubt, be ready in a couple of years but for now they need a bit more time at the coalface, so to speak. Tony Dean, the other consultant, had a massive heart attack and it really had a knock-on effect in the department. Morale dropped, stress levels went up. I had a long discussion with Sam and he talked me into taking the job—he can be very persuasive when he wants to be.'

'How does he cope, being the only consultant? It must be a huge strain.'

Fay nodded. 'It is. Hopefully they'll find a suitable temporary replacement for Tony soon. They're interviewing next week. Sam needs a break, that's for sure.'

Erin couldn't resist going further. 'He said his mother was very sick,' she commented, rather too lightly. 'That can't help matters much.'

Fay raised her eyebrows. 'My, my, he has been opening up. What did you do? Hypnotise him with that crystal to drag a good story out of him?'

Erin managed to laugh. 'We were just talking. Off the record,' she added, 'as we are now.'

Fay's face suddenly grew serious. 'We all joke about this place sending us to an early grave, but I tell you now—it's too much for one man. He might be officially off at seven tonight but we all know that if something big comes in or something goes wrong, the registrar on call will have to ring Sam. And I'm not exaggerating when I say that happens most days and nights. Make sure you put that in when you put your piece together. It's all very well for Admin to demand changes and the press to jump on our backs, but there's only so much that can be done, and Sam is doing far more than any one person should have to.'

Erin heard the genuine concern in Fay's voice and it unnerved her. How much could one man take?

'It's a shame he's not in a relationship. I mean…' Erin flushed under Fay's scrutiny. 'I wasn't putting my hand up or anything. It was just something he said.'

'Strictly off the record?' Fay asked, and Erin nodded eagerly.

'Go for it. A happy, dizzy thing like you might be just what the doctor ordered.'

Erin fiddled with her necklace, embarrassed at the way the conversation had turned out yet pleased all the same that Fay didn't think it was too unlikely. 'He'd never look at someone like me in a million years. Anyway, I've only known him a week.'

'Do you think love pays attention to irrelevancies like that? Look, I may be speaking out of turn, and I'm definitely speaking off my own bat, but call it a nurse's intuition—call it what you like. Sam has been the most relaxed I've seen him in ages with you around. Now, considering you come with your own camera crew, that's a fairly big statement. I've been trying to play matchmaker for Sam for years and he's never even given me the faintest hint that he's interested in anyone—until now, that is.'

Erin gulped. 'So you think I should give it a shot?'

Fay shrugged. 'I've said more than enough already. I'd better get home and feed the hubby. Jot down your number and I'll give you a ring.'

Erin scribbled down her number happily, glad to keep a link, however tenuous, with this wonderful place.

'Right, then, I'm off. Enjoy the rest of your evening.' Fay gave a small wink as she made her way to the doors.

'Fay,' Erin called. 'You forgot the roster—you don't want a wasted journey.'

Fay laughed. 'The roster will still be there when I come on duty tonight. I've accomplished all that I intended. I'll catch you later.' And with a cheery wave she was gone, leaving Erin standing in the middle of Resus grinning like a Cheshire cat.

Though the wait must have been interminable for Mr Reed's family, who had gathered in the interview room, despite her fatigue, the last few hours in the department flew by for Erin. Suddenly the hands on the clock were leaping forward in bounds and as Jeremy Foster appeared to inform the family that Mr Reed was in Recovery and awaiting transfer to Intensive Care, seven o'clock came and went. Jeremy caught her eye as he left the family.

'Bet you wish you'd taken me up on my offer to come up to Theatre now.'

Erin smiled. 'Far too gory for me, but I'm glad it all went well.'

Jeremy grinned. 'Great, wasn't it?'

Erin could hear the genuine relief in his voice, and then he added in more familiar tones, 'I'd have hated to have had a death on national television.' Jeremy glanced at his watch. 'I was supposed to be somewhere half an hour ago, so I'd better go. It was nice meeting you.'

Erin shook his hand. 'Make sure you've got a blank tape ready for next Sunday night.'

With a smile and a wave, Jeremy walked off. Erin found herself smiling. He wasn't all bad and she'd grown fond of him. She thought of how he had nervously explained things to Mr Reed and in his own way tried to comfort him. Despite his vanity and lack of social skill, he obviously was a good surgeon.

Mark had arrived back at the hospital a couple of hours ago, and now he came over. 'Don't suppose you're up to going over things tonight?'

Erin shook her head. 'I'm exhausted. Where's the camera crew?'

'Out the doors on the stroke of seven. I wanted to get a shot of Mr Reed in Intensive Care, but we'd have been heading into overtime.'

'Oh, well, it might be a nice idea just to leave it hanging, show how nothing here fits into a time slot.'

Mark nodded. 'Good idea, we'll go over it tomorrow. You'll be in, of course?'

'Try and keep me away.' She watched as Mark yawned hugely. 'Maybe you should go back to bed.'

'Don't worry, I'm going. Do you want to share a taxi?'

Erin thought for a moment. Looking around, she watched as everyone carried on with their business—the porters pushing a gurney, the domestic mopping the floor, the nurses rushing around, only pausing to stop a moment as they passed the whiteboard, Samuel talking on the telephone. For a second he looked up. Holding her gaze, he gave her a slow, slightly questioning smile.

'You go on, Mark. I might just stay and say thanks to everyone.'

'But you'll be seeing them tomorrow and, no doubt, most of next week. You've still got your intro to film and there'll be loads of re-asks.'

But Erin had made up her mind. 'No, really. You go.'

He hadn't even made it out of the doors before Samuel came over. 'You all done, then?'

'For now, yes. The real work starts tomorrow.'

Samuel hesitated for a moment. 'I'm nearly done here. Would you like to wait for me? We could—' He never got to finish his sentence because at that moment Vicki rushed up, obviously upset.

'Can I have a word, Sam?'

He took her arm and led her away from Erin. As she watched she saw Samuel's face grow pale. Something terrible must have happened. Vicki rushed off and Samuel went to follow, then briefly he turned. 'I'm sorry, I'm going to be here a while. You'd better go.'

'Is something wrong?'

For a second he didn't answer, and when he did his voice was quiet and Erin felt the hairs on the back of her neck stand on end as he delivered the bad news. 'Jeremy Foster has been in a motor smash. It doesn't sound too good. They're bringing him in shortly. It's going to be pretty heavy down here for a while.'

'But he was just here. It couldn't have been more than fifteen minutes ago. I was talking to him...'

Samuel took a deep breath and closed his eyes. 'Fifteen minutes is all it takes.' He rubbed his furrowed forehead with his fingers. 'Erin, I have to go.'

He didn't wait for her to respond, and Erin watched as a mass of doctors in white coats and theatre greens started to make their way into the resuscitation room, each desperate to lend their skills in the battle to save one of their own. She listened as Samuel directed them out. 'Only the trauma team, guys. Too many people around will only create more problems. We'll keep you all informed.'

Again he caught Erin's eye as she stood there, surveying the scene. She didn't want to leave. For whatever reason, she wanted to stay, to see how Jeremy was, to see how they coped. And, she admitted to herself, to see how Samuel was afterwards. But what could she offer? They were the ones with the expertise. She was merely a reporter, and her allocated time slot was over. What right did she have to be upset? After all, she had only known Jeremy Foster for a couple of days.

She knew she should ring Mark and tell him what had happened. It was news after all, and made all the more interesting by the amount of footage they had of Jeremy. She could almost see the headline now, but somehow she couldn't do it. Mark would have to wait for his story.

As she made her way to collect her bag, suddenly it

all became clear. It didn't matter that her time at the hospital had only been short. It had taken only these few days to turn her life around. She loved it here, and she loved the staff. And, more importantly, she loved Samuel Donovan.

CHAPTER EIGHT

LETTING herself into her house, Erin picked up a note from the mantelpiece. Though she desperately wanted to go over the weekend, to share her experiences, she was actually glad when she read that Anna was staying with Jordan. Anna simply wouldn't understand. She toyed with the idea of ringing Fay but, looking at the clock, realised that she would be getting ready for work now. Instead, she poured her heart out to Hartley. His big brown eyes stared dolefully into hers as she told him about her weekend, about Fay and Vicki and Jeremy and finally Samuel.

'I'm sure he was going to ask me out, Hartley, positive.' But Hartley didn't reply, of course. The ringing of the phone made her jump. For a second she had the wildest notion it might be Samuel, ringing to tell her how Jeremy was doing. But why would he ring her? she reasoned. How could he realise how much it had upset her? He would just assume it was simply anther job to her.

'Did you see the news?' Mark's excited voice infuriated her.

'I haven't turned the television on yet,' she answered casually. She wasn't going to let on that she knew already.

'That slick surgeon only went and smashed his Porsche outside the hospital gates. It's a shame the cameras weren't around. We could have got some great shots. Still, I've rung the office and they're putting together a report. Hopefully we can release his name by the late news and show some of the footage we've got of him.'

Erin listened silently, fuming as he ranted on. Mark obviously couldn't care less about what had happened to Jeremy—all he was interested in was the story.

'Hold onto your hat, Erin. With this much publicity, next Sunday night is going to be a ratings winner! We've got the Graysons' surprise delivery on tonight's news, along with the surgeon's accident. It couldn't have worked out better.'

'Have you heard how he is?' Erin's voice was strained but Mark didn't notice.

'Who?'

'Jeremy,' she wailed.

Mark answered dismissively 'By all accounts he's in a pretty bad way—head and spinal injuries or something.' He gave a small laugh. 'He wanted to get his face on television, but I bet he wasn't banking on making the national news tonight.'

It wasn't Mark's fault, she knew that deep down. He dealt with news stories every day and so did she. You'd go crazy if you got involved personally with each one. But she *was* involved, she knew that now. The whole weekend had been far more than just a story to her. Somehow she managed some small talk with Mark, she even shared a laugh, but as she replaced the telephone Erin felt sick. She simply had to know more. Shakingly she retrieved her work notes and dialled the hospital number.

'Melbourne City Hospital. Can I help you?'

'Could you put me through to the nurses' station in Accident and Emergency?'

She held her breath as the telephone rang.

'Sister Jenny Barton speaking,'

Erin swallowed hard. It was the young nurse who had dealt with Mr Reed. 'It's Erin Casey here. I was wondering if I might enquire how Jeremy Foster is doing. They were just bringing him in as I left.'

She strained her ears as Jenny called out to someone. 'It's another reporter on the telephone. Wants an update on Jeremy.'

The words tore through her, but at the end of the day that was all she was to them—a reporter. The unit was busy enough without catering to her thirst for knowledge. She wanted to say that wasn't why she had rung. That her interest was genuine. But what was the point? What did they care?

A crisp voice Erin didn't recognise came to the telephone and she listened quietly as the usual spiel reserved for the press was given out. The doctor in question was critically ill, and the hospital had no further comment. They would appreciate it if his name could be withheld at this stage until all relatives had been informed.

She could have found out as much by turning on the television.

Wearily she ran a bath, adding a large dash of aromatic oils. For once the fragrances did nothing to soothe her, but she still lay there until the water was cold and her skin had shrivelled. Making her way down the stairs, Erin stiffened as through the hall window she saw a dark figure making its way up the garden path. But her nerves vanished in an instant as she recognised the wide set of the shoulders even in the darkness.

She took the final three stairs in one quick leap and even before he had knocked she was wrestling with the lock on the heavy front door. Only as she opened it did she stop to think of her appearance—wrapped in a flimsy silk robe, her hair still damp from the bath, with absolutely no make-up. Samuel seemed too preoccupied to care about her appearance, though a tired smile lit his face as he entered the hallway.

'I saw a light on. I'm sorry, I know it's late…'

She swept away his apologies. 'I couldn't even think of going to bed. I've been so worried about Jeremy. I even tried to ring the hospital but they just gave me the usual update.' She gibbered on, suddenly flustered. 'But why *are* you here? I thought you'd seen enough of me to last a lifetime after the last twenty-four hours.'

Samuel didn't reply. Instead, he gestured towards the living room and when Erin nodded he made his way through, sitting heavily on the sofa. He leant back against the cushion, closing his eyes, and she watched as he smothered a yawn. He was still dressed in theatre greens. His blond hair seemed darker and there were heavy rings under his eyes, yet he was still the most beautiful thing she had ever seen.

'You must be exhausted,' she said sympathetically. 'Can I get you a drink?'

'Later maybe.' He looked around for a moment before his eyes found her. 'I don't really know what I'm doing here. I knew you'd be worried about Jeremy and we never did get to finish our conversation.'

Erin nodded, slightly breathless, as he continued, 'I was going to see if you wanted to come out for a drink, sort of a debriefing session.' He gave a small laugh. 'Who am I trying to kid? I wanted to see you, full stop.' His eyes seemed to be burning into her as he stared at her longingly. 'Does that worry you?'

In a second she was beside him. 'It's the best thing anyone's ever said to me,' she answered with an appealing honesty. 'I'm so glad you came.'

Erin thought she would faint with desire as his rough,

unshaven face met hers, his heavy lips finding hers with an urgency she knew only too well. All the pent-up emotion and frustration that had bought them to this tender moment dissolved as they sensually explored each other with their mouths, affirming their mutual desire for each other in a slow unhurried kiss. As they gently pulled away their eyes stayed locked together, as if seeing each other for the first time.

'I've been wanting to do that from the moment I saw you in Admin,' he confessed.

The fact he had felt it, too, that he had wanted her as much as she had wanted him, was almost overwhelming. With a sigh she leant her head onto his broad chest and rested there a moment, breathing in his maleness, revelling in the tight embrace of his powerful arms. Never had she felt so right, so safe, so wanted. Opening her eyes suddenly, shame swept over her and she sat bolt upright.

'But I never even asked—how is Jeremy?'

Samuel pulled her back into his arms and she lay there as he stroked her hair and told her gently the terrible news.

'It isn't good. He's very sick.'

'Mark said he had spinal injuries,' she mentioned gently. She felt the tension in him beneath her.

'I think he'll be all right from that point of view. At first we were worried he'd broken his neck but his X-rays were clear. He's got a lot of internal injuries, though, and he's still in Theatre. The main worry is his head injury. It doesn't look too good.'

'Will he live—I mean, as far as you can tell?'

Samuel carried on stroking her hair as she spoke and she lay listening as large tears rolled onto his chest. 'I don't know,' he said honestly, and his voice was thick with emotion. 'I'm pretty sure they can fix his internal injuries, but his head injury is the unknown entity. He's got a skull fracture and cerebral oedama, so basically it's wait and see. Put it this way, if he does live he's not going to be back at work in the next couple of weeks. He's got a long road ahead of him.'

'It's so unfair,' Erin wept. 'I mean, I know I hardly know him, I know it's far worse for you. But he just seemed so...' She struggled to find the words. 'So confident, so alive. So clever.'

'So vain.'

She smiled through her tears. 'That, too. I still liked him.'

He kissed the top of her head. 'I like him, too. But I wouldn't write Jeremy off too quickly. He's a stubborn guy, that's for sure, and there's no way he's going to miss himself on television if he's got any say in the matter.' He pulled her up to face him and she could see the pain etched in his features as he spoke. 'You never know what's around the corner. It's a cliché, I know, but one I repeat every day, working in A and E. You can make all these plans, have all these dreams—and for what? Sometimes you just have to seize the moment and to hell with the consequences because, who knows? You might never get another chance.'

She didn't answer, watching transfixed as he spoke. Samuel winced and she knew he was recalling some of the things he had seen. She put a hand up to his face and he held it there against his unshaven cheek as he spoke in heavy, pain-filled tones.

'God, it was hard, seeing him like that. I know I've sometimes moaned like crazy about him and we've had our share of arguments...' He shook his head and she knew he was struggling to keep his composure. 'I'm not a betting man but, between Jeremy and I, I'd have put my house on me ending up in a wheelchair or worse before him. Seeing him like that, lying there on that resuscitation bed…'

So intent was Erin on trying to comfort him, and so heady was she from the effect of lying so close to him, that she missed the poignancy of his words. Missed the chance to somehow avoid the terrible mess that was about to unravel. 'You did your best,' she said simply. 'You did your best.' She gave him a gentle kiss. 'What you need is a massage,' she added brightly, but Samuel screwed up his nose at the suggestion.

'I'm not in labour,' he said sarcastically, but Erin could sense weakness.

'Come on. You always knock my suggestions. Why don't you give it a try and then you can judge me? I'm not trying to seduce you.'

Samuel raised a quizzical eyebrow. 'I don't mind if you are, but I'm not having a massage.'

'It would really help. Please, at least let me try.' Erin was nothing if not persistent, a born nag maybe, and she carried on incessantly until finally and somewhat amazingly she managed to get him to reluctantly agree.

'You'll have me sitting under a tripod next,' he moaned as hesitantly he stripped out of his greens and she placed a towel over him to preserve his modesty.

'Now, just close your eyes and try to think of nothing.'

'Easier said than done.'

'Then just think of something nice.'

Erin poured some oil into her palms, rubbing them together to warm the oil and release the fragrance. Despite her insistence that it was purely a massage, she couldn't ignore the electric charge that coursed through her as her oiled hands met his skin. Swallowing hard, she tried to concentrate on her rhythm, her hands rubbing his back with rhythmic firm strokes, her nimble fingers soothing away the knots of tension around his neck. And gradually under her touch he finally relaxed, groaning slightly as she found a particularly tense muscle.

'See, I told you it helped,' she whispered as she carried on, pouring some more oil into her hands and moved herself slightly lower to work on his legs. Suddenly the room seemed to have shrunk in size. She swallowed hard as she placed her hands on his thighs. Thick and muscular, the blond hairs were light against his deep tan, and Erin knew she had set herself an impossible task, for how could she touch him and not convey how much she desired him? He seemed to sense her hesitancy and she felt him tense beneath her touch. He rolled onto his back, his hand reaching for the towel to cover himself.

'I thought you said you weren't trying to seduce me?' His voice was thick with lust and she couldn't meet his eyes. She placed her oiled hands on his chest, the same silken blond hair darkening under her oiled fingers, his nipples firm beneath her touch. She knew she was being bold, she knew it was too soon, but right here, right now, it simply didn't matter. His hands skilfully undid the loose knot of her robe and she brazenly pulled away the towel, gasping as she saw him lying there naked before her.

Her soft hands slowly explored the delicious velvety steel length of his malehood, slipping through her fingers with a life of its own. She lowered her head and buried her face in the soft blond down. She could feel her breasts brushing against his thighs, his hands burrowing into her hair as she explored him with her warm tongue. Gasping with pleasure, he pulled her up, his muscular arms sliding her petite frame along his oiled body until her face was level with his. She could feel him unbridled between her legs, feel his aching urgency, and without a murmur she lifted her hips, allowing his hands to skilfully guide her down.

The piercing pleasure as she lowered herself caused a groan to escape from her parted lips. She was as oiled and welcoming as he was and he slipped inside, his hips grinding against her thighs as she bucked against him. One hand reaching up, he massaged her swollen breasts while the other held the peach of her buttocks, steadying her as she moved with him. She felt him swell within as she gripped him tightly, her own body tensing as they climaxed together, holding each other as time stood still. Breathless, exhausted, she relaxed against him and tenderly he guided her down to the floor beside him. Enfolding her in her arms, he pulled a throw rug over them and they lay there, her head on his chest, listening as his rapid heartbeat gradually slowed down.

There was no need for words as they lay there together. No need for explanations or justification for their actions. Instead, as they lay entwined there was a gentle acceptance, a mutual unspoken affirmation of the desire they both had shared. And despite the fact she had only known him a short while, despite the logical reasons for waiting, Erin felt no shame at what had transpired, no regrets for surrendering herself so easily to him. For how, she fathomed, could she repent something so beautiful and natural as the love they had shared?

Erin, sometimes to her credit but mostly to her detriment, always managed to say exactly what was on her mind. And as her endorphin-induced haze slowly lifted and the reality of what had transpired slowly drifted in, the words escaped from her lips even before she had lucidly thought them.

'We didn't use any protection,' she blurted, sitting up

suddenly. 'I mean, I'm not on the Pill or anything. I wasn't expecting to...' There was no master plan intended, no secret desire for him to pull her into his arms and whisper platitudes that they would face come what may together. But if a crack squad of armed police had suddenly invaded the house Samuel's reaction couldn't have been more dramatic. Pulling back the throw rug, he stood up, grabbing at his discarded clothes as Erin watched in stunned silence, blinking in the darkness as he hastily dressed.

'I have to go,' he uttered, more to himself than to her.

'Now? But surely...' Her voice trailed off as she searched his face for a clue to his abrupt change.

He didn't meet her eyes. 'I ought to get back to the hospital.' His voice was clear, his statement reasonable. She knew he was busy, knew he was needed, but Erin knew deep down he was also lying.

'Samuel, please.' Her voice bore a hint of desperation as she grabbed the rug around her, standing up to try to reason with him.

'I said, I have to go.' The tones were the same ones he had used before back in A and E when he was the doctor and she was the lowly reporter. It was as if nothing had ever happened between them.

How Erin would have loved to have been one of those women who could shrug nonchalantly, who could suppress their feelings and retain their composure in the face of adversity. But it simply wasn't Erin. With an angry sob she lunged at him, grabbing his arm as he went to walk out, her anger and desperation fuelling a surge of energy in her tiny frame which, temporarily at least, seemed to restrain him.

'Samuel, you can't just come here, make love to me and then leave me like this. You can't do this to me.'

Her voice held all the angst she was feeling and for a moment it held him. Slowly he turned, listening as she continued passionately, 'What sort of woman do you take me for?'

Finally his eyes met hers, as if somehow her words had reached him. 'Erin, I'm so sorry.' She watched as he lowered himself onto the sofa, placing his elbows on his knees and resting his head in his hands. He stared at the floor for an age as she stood there, shivering with mortification, the flimsy rug no barrier to the emotions coursing through her.

He took a deep, steadying breath before he dragged his eyes to meet hers. 'I shouldn't have come. I had no intention of…well, what happened.'

His face was filled with a pain she had never witnessed but she was too confused and too emotional to even try to comfort him. 'Then why did you?' she managed to rasp.

He didn't reply.

Pulling the rug more tightly around her, she spoke more firmly. 'Samuel, why did you?'

'Because I wanted to see you. I never should have let things go so far. What we did was a mistake.'

His damning words ripped through her. 'No!' She was almost shouting now. 'How can you say that? ''What we did''?' Her voice was rising now. 'We made love, Samuel, that's what we did. And it was beautiful and wonderful—you know it was. Don't you dare try and cheapen it now.'

But he was already slipping away and Erin knew it. This time when he stood up to leave she didn't try to stop him.

'It can't happen again. I'm sorry if I hurt you—that was never my intention, you have to believe that.'

As he made his way into the hallway, she found her voice. Her words seemed to echo as she called to his departing back, 'I don't know what to believe, Samuel.'

He didn't respond. Didn't turn around and try to offer an explanation. Instead, he gently closed the front door behind him as Erin stood there, stunned and shell-shocked. It was all she could do to climb the stairs and throw herself onto her bed, clutching the rug close to her, smelling his heady fragrance. It was the only tangible proof, apart from her broken heart, that he had even been.

CHAPTER NINE

SOMEHOW Erin limped through the next few days. But
there was no escape from her pain, no refuge or solace
to be found. Samuel filled her dreams at night and there
was no reprieve during the day as her time was spent
editing the report. His face was everywhere, freeze
frames of his strong profile, and she devoured each one,
scanning each image, searching—for what, she didn't
know. There was footage she hadn't seen before and she
tried to watch it objectively. To somehow obliterate the
emotion that engulfed her as she watched him work, as
unattainable on her screen as he was in real life. But it
was useless. She wanted to preserve everything. Pushing
the delete button was a feat in itself.

'What's this?' she asked as Mark came into the room
with some coffee.

He looked up at the monitor and grinned. 'It's anything
you want it to be.'

Erin swallowed hard and turned back to the monitor.
Images of empty beds on the medical ward filled the
screen. The shots of the clock had been captured, too.
Nurses were sitting at the nurses' station, idly flicking
through magazines.

'When did you get this?' she asked slowly.

'When we followed a patient up to the ward, remember? Just before that drunk-driver came in.'

Erin didn't reply. Mark was right. These images could
be anything she wanted them to be. She recalled the conversation she'd had with Samuel. How the press and the

public didn't understand about bed availability. He was right, of course. And these pictures, taken out of context, could be damning.

'Did you get a shot of the empty bed in Coronary Care?' Her voice was strangely high.

'You're learning fast, darling. Carry on watching.'

An image of the coronary care entrance came onto the screen. They hadn't managed to film the empty bed but they had a shot of the eight monitors at the nurses' station—seven filled with tracings, one screen darkened. It was all that was needed to show there was a vacant bed.

Revenge would have been sweet. To say she wasn't tempted would have been a lie. But Erin wasn't a naturally vindictive person. Anyway, to do a hatchet job on the department couldn't begin to make up for the pain she felt. All it would do would be to cause further misery.

'We're not going to go there, Mark.'

'Why not? This is dynamite…'

'It's inaccurate. Samuel explained the reasoning behind not using the beds.'

'On film? Where?'

Erin shook her head 'We talked about it. There were very good reasons why Elsie White wasn't transferred up to the ward. We should be explaining them, educating the public, not just going in with all guns blazing for the sake of creating a bit of drama.'

But Mark was having none of it. He sensed she was wavering and pushed harder. 'There's a lot of interest in this show. The ratings are going to be the highest yet. You've got a chance to make a name for yourself. A simpy story about how pushed the staff are isn't going to do that, Erin. If you want the follow-on publicity, if you want MPs using this in the run-up to the election, you're going to have to make some waves.'

But Erin stood resolute. Her voice was clearer now, more certain. 'No, we've got enough drama without making it up. That's not what I want this piece to be about. It will stand on its own merits without sensationalising the bed situation. We could actually do some good here, Mark, can't you see that? We can still show the beds, but explain the reasoning behind the decisions.'

Mark took a drink of his coffee and looked at her consideringly. 'You're a fool, then, Erin Casey.' He sat down at his screen and angrily started tapping away as Erin sat there, her face burning.

She might be a fool, a big one to think that Samuel Donovan could ever really have cared about her, to have fallen into his arms and given him all too easily, but she wasn't going to lower herself this way. She still had her integrity, professionally anyway. Making no attempt to break the uncomfortable silence, Erin turned to her own screen. Repeating the words to herself, she started to tap away. She still had her professional integrity. For a moment her hands hovered above the keys as an image of Samuel as clear as the ones caught on film invaded her mind, and she had to swallow hard to fight the tears that were threatening. How, she wondered for the millionth time, could she have read him so wrong?

Had she been hoping for some feminine insight, some moral support or even a glass of wine and some sympathy, she wasn't going to be getting it from Anna.

'You mean you slept with him?' The horror in her voice as Anna turned and stared, aghast, made Erin question the wisdom behind opening up to her sister. 'But you hardly know him! Erin, how could you?'

Erin shook her head fiercely. 'I know I haven't known him for long, but from the moment we saw each other there was an attraction, there really was, Anna,' Erin insisted as her sister gave her a disbelieving look. 'Honestly, the time we shared together was so special, we really connected. You said yourself what a great guy he was.'

'Oh, come on, Erin,' Anna snorted. 'I didn't mean you to jump into bed with him. Oh, excuse me,' she continued sarcastically, 'you didn't get that far, did you? The lounge room floor had to suffice.'

Erin put her hands up to her ears. 'Don't make it sound sordid, like some sort of one-night stand,' she begged. 'It truly wasn't like that.'

'Well, then, where is he?'

Erin swallowed hard, Anna's words lacerating her. It was the one question she didn't have an answer to, and it was the one question that summed it all up.

'If it wasn't a one night stand, just where is he now?' Anna continued relentlessly, ignoring the tears that were sliding down Erin's cheeks. 'For goodness' sake, Erin, it's time you grew up. How can you expect Samuel to respect you when you don't respect yourself? Now, if you'll excuse me, I'm not feeling the best. I'm going to bed.'

Erin bit her lip as Anna walked out. To Anna, life was black and white. She had been stupid to even hope that Anna could ever understand the wave of emotion that she and Samuel had been caught up in. How could Anna even begin to fathom the passion and aura that had surrounded them that beautiful night? It would be easy to retaliate and start a row—to throw a couple of shots about how boring she and Jordan were, how there was a world outside Jordan's work—but what would it achieve? Jordan and Anna were happy. Just because it wasn't what suited Erin, it didn't mean it was wrong. Still, she *was* disappointed. Just because Anna didn't understand or approve of what had happened with Samuel, surely she could have been a little more compassionate?

But Anna obviously thought that taking the moral high ground was merited and the strained atmosphere at home only exacerbated the utter misery Erin was feeling. The only positive thing in her life for once was work. At least there, everything seemed to be coming together beautifully. Each newsbreak advertised Sunday night's show, with hints of the dramas to come. Newspapers were picking up the story, and some of the bigwigs were even nodding to Erin in the corridor.

She simultaneously dreaded and yearned to go back to A and E to do the re-asks and introduction. Over and over Erin rehearsed what she would say when she ran into Samuel. Hating herself for being so materialistic, she blew a week's wages on a cream suit. The skirt was daringly short, showing just enough tanned thigh, but the fitted jacket gave her a slight edge. It wasn't exactly power dressing, she insisted to herself as she slipped on some low-heeled court shoes, just a confidence boost. Snipping the price tag off the jacket, she swallowed her guilt. Almost a week's mortgage payment—maybe she should think hard before she spoke to the bank. There'd be no more splurges like this if she bought Anna out. Oh, but it was worth it, she realised as she stood back and admired her reflection. She could almost pass as a sophisticated— or at the very least a reasonably successful—reporter. She certainly didn't look anything like the emotional wreck Samuel had walked out on last Sunday. At least she had a genuine excuse to speak to him. After all, it was Samuel who had made her promise he could see the show before it was screened. She was only keeping her word.

*   *   *

She would be cool, Erin decided, and friendly as well. But not gushing, definitely not gushing. She wouldn't fish or push. If he wanted to explain or catch up, she'd accept, of course, but not too eagerly. And if she felt a blush coming on, well, she would stare at the white wall over his shoulder until it passed. Simple really!

Her self-imposed orders buzzing in her head, Erin locked her Alfa and made her way over to the department. Pushing open the swing doors, she swallowed hard and forced a smile. And though she had dreaded seeing him, nothing, but nothing could have prepared Erin for the devastation she felt when she realised he wasn't there. Subtly she checked the whiteboard. A name she didn't recognise was at the top. With a surge of hope she considered the possibility that he might just be down at the canteen or having a coffee in the rest room, behind a cubicle curtain maybe, but her intuition was stronger than her hopes. Samuel wasn't here, she just *knew*.

Touchingly, though, the staff were all really pleased to see her and they greeted her like a long-lost friend.

'Erin, you look fabulous.' Fay gave her a warm hug. 'You're not going to point that thing at me again, are you?' she asked, gesturing to Dave who had just walked in.

Erin grinned. 'Hopefully I can spare you. It's just going to be me giving an intro and then I have to do a couple of re-asks.'

Fay gave her a quizzical look.

'I have to film me asking some questions. I'll need to borrow a pair of theatre greens if that's OK.'

Fay smiled. 'Sure, though without the bags under your eyes and the messed-up hair, I don't know how authentic it will look.'

'Don't let my make-up fool you. I'll do the posh bits

first and then I'll go and wash it off. Believe me, Fay, I'll look authentic.'

Fay gave her a sympathetic look. 'Actually, on closer inspection, you do look a bit peaky. Is anything wrong?'

Erin shook her head fiercely. 'I'm fine, just a bit tired. It's always busy towards the end of a big piece,' she said with conviction, but it was wasted on Fay. They both knew this was her first and only big story. Her eyes wandered over the department. Samuel definitely wasn't around and, without needing to be asked, Fay answered her question.

'Sam's not here.' She hesitated. 'He's got a lot going on at the moment.' Fay's eyes didn't quite meet hers and Erin was sure she felt uncomfortable. She must know. How *could* he have told her? Erin felt a huge blush start and quickly averted her eyes to the peeling white-painted wall. Of course Fay knew. She and Samuel were friends after all. Samuel had probably asked Fay to cover for him when she came so he didn't have to see her.

'How's Jeremy Foster?'

Fay gave a relieved look, obviously glad of the change of subject.

'Holding his own. He's still in Intensive Care, but it looks as if he'll make it. He's in for the long haul, though at best he'll need extensive rehabilitation.'

'And at worst?' Erin asked quietly.

'I don't even want to think about it. He'll get there. I just went up this morning and told him we were all missing his pompous attitude and he'd better hurry up and get back to us.'

Erin laughed. 'What did he say to that?'

But the laughter died on her lips as Fay answered seriously. 'He didn't answer, Erin, he's still unconscious— but who knows? Maybe he can hear.'

The two women stood there lost in their thoughts for a moment before Erin broke the silence. 'I'd better get started, then,'

Fay gave a small nod. 'Sure. Help yourself. I'll go and find you some greens.'

Somehow Erin got through her work, even though neither her heart nor mind were in it. Her eyes kept darting to the swing doors as if somehow her longing might make him magically appear. Of course, he didn't. Finally, trying desperately not to linger, Erin said her goodbyes and made her way dejectedly to the car park. She had been through every scenario imaginable, every possible reaction he might have when they finally did meet. For him not to be there was the only outcome she hadn't prepared for.

Halfway to her car Erin gave a small groan. Her bag with her keys was sitting in the staff coffee-room. The afternoon was impossibly hot and muggy and the walk back to A and E seemed inordinately long. Making her way into the staffroom, she stopped abruptly when she saw Fay and Samuel locked in a private conversation. Fay's concerned face looked up as she entered.

'Erin, I thought you'd already gone.'

Samuel had the grace to look embarrassed but didn't say anything, leaving it to Erin to break the uncomfortable silence.

'I got all the way to the car before I realised I'd forgotten my bag.' Her voice was as casual as she could manage as she made her way over to the sofa and retrieved the offending object, painfully aware of a huge blush that simply wouldn't fade. Samuel had obviously been hiding and had left it to Fay to make excuses for him. The second she had gone Fay must have paged him to give him the all-clear. Anger started to build in Erin—

she didn't deserve this. These were two people she had considered at the very least friends. She had confided some of her innermost feelings to them both and they had let her. Now they were treating her as if she were some sort of stalker. Hell, it had been Samuel who had turned up at her house. As she got to the door she turned.

'The final edit should be ready for you to view tomorrow.' When he didn't respond, she added, 'You did make me promise that you could see it.' She reminded him pointedly, so he was under no illusion she was trying to prolong this most uncomfortable meeting.

'I'm going to have to trust you,' he said slowly, as Erin raised a slim eyebrow. 'I've got rather a lot going on.'

Erin looked at him incredulously. Was he that terrified of being alone with her?

'Ah, yes,' she said dryly. 'Fay did say as much.' She opened the door then turned briefly. 'Don't worry, *Mr* Donovan, I won't let *you* down.' It took every last piece of self-control she could muster not to slam the door.

The drive home was a nightmare. Despite the relatively short distance to her home from the hospital, it took for ever. Gripping the steering-wheel tightly, she concentrated on the road. She absolutely would not cry, not yet anyway. The heat was unbearable and Erin looked on enviously at the cars with their windows wound up as she got caught at yet another red light. The next car she got would definitely have air-conditioning. Her linen suit had crumpled and her hair was plastered to her face as she wrestled with the rush-hour traffic. So much for the cool, sophisticated look, she thought wryly as she caught sight of her reflection in the rear-view mirror.

The absence of Anna's Fiat in the driveway came as a relief. She simply wasn't up to any more of her sister's lectures. Letting herself in, she flicked on the air-conditioning, made her way upstairs and gratefully slipped out of her suit. Only when she was safely in the shower, with the jets of cool water aimed directly at her head, did she give in, allowing the tears she had so fiercely held back since that awful meeting with him to finally come. The violence of her feelings and the anguish in her tears surprised even Erin. She had pinned so much on today without realising it. The success of the show seemed almost irrelevant. Everything did now.

How long she stayed in the shower Erin wasn't sure, but the water was running cold and it was a shivering, gulping Erin who wrapped a skimpy towel around herself and searched the bathroom and her bedroom in vain for her bathrobe. The air-conditioning was on full blast and she was positively cold now, something she could only have dreamed of earlier in the car. Anna must have borrowed it. Normally they stayed out of each other's rooms, an almost essential rule when you had two women with such opposite natures living in the same house, but Erin was *freezing* and anyway she would only have a quick peek. Anna wouldn't mind.

The sight that greeted her was one she could never have envisaged. With a strangled scream she surveyed the scene in horror, her hands shooting up to her face as the towel dropped to the floor.

'Anna, no!' She ran over to the bed, her voice catching in her throat. *'No!'*

Anna didn't respond. Her face was grey, her lips tinged blue. She was sitting upright on the bed, supported by a mountain of pillows, her head lolling back. Beside her limp hand lay her Ventolin pump. She was breathing, Erin realised with infinite relief as she knelt beside her, long, laboured breaths with an ominous wheeze.

Instinctively Erin reached for Anna's pump, knowing she had to get the medicine into Anna while she was still breathing, even if only slightly. But as soon as she squeezed it Erin realised it was empty.

'Oh, Anna, you poor thing. Is that what happened?' But Anna didn't make any response.

Erin knew she needed to get help, and quickly. Anna was critically ill, but the telephone was downstairs and she couldn't leave her like this.

'Think, Erin,' she begged of herself. 'Stay calm. What would the girls in A and E do?'

The nebuliser! Never had Erin been more grateful for Anna's pedantic nature. Pulling out the top drawer of the dresser, she saw the small machine exactly where it always was. Plugging it in, she grabbed at the bag containing the plastic ampoules of medication that Anna used when she was particularly bad. Spilling most of it, she nevertheless managed to squeezed some of the drugs into the bowl and attach it to the mask. Flicking on the switch, she watched the white vapour pour from the mask and placed it over Anna's slack face, tightening the green elastic.

Still terrified of leaving her but knowing she desperately needed some help, she ran down the stairs. Not sure if she had charged her mobile and remembering something Vicki had said about the emergency services being unable to trace mobile calls, she used the home telephone. It took only seconds to answer but it seemed like an eternity. The calm voice asking which service she required calmed her for a second.

'Ambulance, quickly.'

Somehow she recited her address, gave the details of the emergency and told them what she had done.

'Give her continuous Ventolin until the paramedics get there.'

'I need to get back upstairs to her. She's on her own, she might have stopped breathing.'

'Do you know CPR?'

Erin closed her eyes. The thought of having to perform CPR on her own sister was abhorrent, but she was infinitely grateful for the course her company had reluctantly sent her on.

'Yes,' she managed to gasp. 'I have to go.'

'Open the front door first, and don't hang up the telephone. They're on their way.'

Taking the stairs three and four at a time, Erin raced back up. Anna was still breathing, but only just. There was nothing, nothing Erin could do except refill the bowl with more medication and wait and pray.

'I love you, Anna,' she said, taking her sister's cold hand in hers. 'Don't you go and leave me. I need you.'

The distant wail of the sirens cutting through the evening air was the only sound Erin wanted to hear. As the wail drew closer, she kissed Anna's soft cheek. 'Hang in there, Anna.'

Stunned and shaking, she watched with a mixture of relief and terror as the paramedics worked on the only person she really had left in the world.

They were practised and efficient and obviously knew what they were doing—but did they realise just how precious Anna was? That she was all Erin had?

'I'm coming with her,' Erin said firmly as they loaded her sister's limp body onto the stretcher. Monitors and tubes seemed to be coming from everywhere.

'We need to get her to hospital quickly. There won't be room in the back of the ambulance—I'll be working on her.' The paramedic spoke kindly but authoritatively. She had a gentle face and Erin was reminded of Fay.

'I want to go with her,' she begged.

But the paramedic shook her head firmly. 'You make your own way in the car, or get a neighbour or taxi to drive you. We don't want you having an accident. Get yourself dressed and then come. We're taking her to Melbourne City Hospital.'

Reluctantly Erin nodded, tears blurring her eyes as they started to move Anna out of the bedroom. Only then did she realise that she was still naked.

For the millionth time she berated her lack of organisation. Pulling on a pair of shorts and a T-shirt, Erin didn't even attempt to find her sandals, but knew if she wanted to get out of the driveway she at least needed her keys.

'Think, think.' She tried in her bag, in the kitchen, by the phone, and eventually had to resort to retracing her footsteps. It worked, for once. There they were, under the beastly cream suit on the shower floor.

Taking a deep breath once she'd belted herself into her car, she started the engine. Jeremy's accident, her parent's untimely death, the paramedic's warning—all these served to make her drive carefully, but if there were speed cameras on the way to the hospital, Erin acknowledged that she was probably a few hundred dollars the poorer.

Parking, she ran the short distance to the A and E entrance, bypassing Reception and bursting breathlessly through the familiar black swing doors. It was Jenny Barton who came over first.

'You can't just come in here,' she said, making her way over. 'Oh.' She stopped when she saw who it was. 'You're the journalist that was here, aren't you?'

'My sister, she was just bought in,' Erin gasped.

'What's her name?'

'Anna, Anna Casey.'

Jenny screwed up her eyebrows. 'I don't recall seeing her. Did you check the waiting room?'

Erin fought with the urge to grab Jenny by the lapels of her shirt and shake the information out of her.

'She's having an asthma attack—she can't speak, she's unconscious.' She was shouting now and she watched as Jenny's face suddenly registered the connection.

'That's your sister? She went straight into Resus.'

Without pausing to respond, Erin made her way over to the resuscitation area, but Jenny was too quick for her. 'You can't go in there, not yet.' Jenny pulled her back. 'Erin, you know you can't. Come on, wait in here and I'll try to get someone to come and talk to you.'

Erin knew Jenny was right, but it was simply all too much and as the nurse opened the door to the interview room the full horror of what was taking place suddenly hit her. The cold hand of fear that gripped at her heart as she saw the tiny waiting room was all too much to bear. Her hysterical screams filled the department as she turned to run.

'I can't go in there, I can't.' Jenny was blocking the door and Erin pushed her aside in a desperate bid to escape the confines of the interview room. The room where you waited for bad news. The room where you were told your loved ones were never coming home again.

'That's where they tell you they're dead,' she sobbed. Her flailing limbs were suddenly caught in a vice-like grip and a deep, familiar voice broke through the screams.

'Easy, Erin, easy.'

And she was in Samuel's arms, her strangled sobs muffled by his solid chest. Large, firm hands caressed her heaving shoulders, gentle comforting words soothed her fears.

Despite Anna being the only thing on her mind, Erin knew she was in the right place, in Samuel's arms where she belonged, where nothing terrible could happen and nothing could go wrong. For a fraction of a second she leant against him, allowed herself the luxury of the comfort of his embrace, the familiar scent of his maleness. And this time when he gently pushed her away she knew it was with good reason.

'I have to go to her now.'

Terrified, blinded by tears, she nodded silently.

'But I'll come and speak to you as soon as I can.' His tone changed as he turned to Jenny who was watching with undisguised interest. 'Go and relieve Vicki in the plaster room and tell her to take Erin into the staffroom and stay with her.'

Jenny nodded but made no attempt to follow his instructions. His arms were still loosely around Erin and her head was still resting on his chest. She felt anger in him rise at Jenny's inaction. 'Now!' he ordered, and Jenny finally scuttled off.

Gulping, sobbing, Erin managed to focus on his face. 'Go,' she gasped. Though she had never needed anyone so much as she needed Samuel now, she knew Anna needed him more.

The clock made a loud clicking sound with every minute that passed. As the red second hand passed the twelve, the big black hand moved forward a fraction and the clock gave a loud click. It was funny, the things you never noticed. Last weekend she had insisted the cameras be focused on the same clock and she had spent the week looking at the hands on the face, making sure it all tied in, and yet only now had she realised just how noisy it was. Perhaps she should ring Mark, tell him to include it. Had Mrs Reed noticed the same monotonous click as the moments ticked by, agonisingly slowly? Had Elsie's relatives thought the same as they'd waited for their mother to get a bed? Were Jeremy's parents thinking it now as they sat in the intensive care unit and waited for their son to regain consciousness?

Vicki was, of course, marvellous. Used to grief, used to dealing with shocked and stunned relatives, she helped with the complicated task of tracing Jordan who had, it turned out, been sent to Sydney by his office for a meeting. Telling him was agonising and not made any easier by the accusing tone Erin was sure she could hear in his voice.

Erin was so grateful for the insight Samuel had shown when he had sent Jenny to get Vicki, and proud also that the staff here in this crazy, wonderful place were treating her like one of their own.

Each time the door opened Erin jumped, sure it must be news of Anna, but each time it was only a staff member grabbing a quick drink or smoke between patients or retrieving something from their locker. But finally, when the night staff started to drift in, their smiles when they initially saw her rapidly disappearing as they heard the circumstances that had bought Erin here, Samuel came into the staffroom. Instantly the chattering stopped and everyone turned to face him.

He made his way over to the sofa where she sat. Erin dragged her eyes up to meet his, terrified what she might see. Though his face was serious, with a flicker of hope Erin knew her sister wasn't dead. Samuel took both her hands and pulled Erin to her feet. 'We'll go into my office.'

'She's all right?' Erin begged, but he didn't reply. Instead, he put a solid arm around her and led her through the full staffroom out into the department and across the unit into his office. Once in there, when the door had closed behind them and they were away from the friendly but prying eyes, he took her into his arms, as if somehow he could act as a buffer for the harsh words she was about to hear as he held her tiny frame to his and gently, painfully took her through what had happened.

'She's very sick, Erin,' he said gently, and she nodded into his chest. 'When she came to us she was barely breathing. She was very difficult to intubate. Anna had a pneumothorax—one of her lungs had collapsed.'

'Would that have caused the asthma?' she gulped against him.

'No, it would have happened as a result of the attack. We had to put a chest tube in to expand the lung. We've given her some hydrocortisone, which takes a while to kick in, and she's on some very strong intravenous drugs. We're waiting for a bed to become available on ICU. It might be a while, though. They're having to do a bit of a bed shuffle.'

'Is she going to die?' It was the worst question she had ever had to ask, but with Samuel there Erin knew she was ready for the truth.

He didn't answer straight away. Instead, he led her to a chair and gently sat her down. Crouching in front of her, he took her hands in his. 'I can't give guarantees and Anna's too sick to be certain but, no, Erin, I don't think so. I think you got to her just in time. We have to be positive.'

As she looked up into his tired, strained face, the temp-

tation to touch him was too much to resist. She lifted one
of her hands and gently touched his face, the rough five-
o'clock shadow scratching her palm as he caught her
hand and for a brief moment rested against it. Closing
his eyes for an instant, he took a deep breath as if her
touch was somehow needed. And Erin just *knew* that it
was. That despite the self-imposed barriers he had so
forcibly erected, despite the cruel end to their love-
making and despite the dearth of answers to her mountain
of questions, Erin was certain that Samuel needed her as
much as she needed him.

CHAPTER TEN

ERIN got to know the intensive care waiting room very well over the next couple of days. The hot-water urn that dripped onto the Laminex if you didn't pull the red knob back just right. The couch that looked so comfortable but was far too low and gave you a stiff back if you dozed off in it was, she learnt, better bypassed for the more formidable straight-backed cane chair. Erin read each one of the leaflets that told her about the various support available to relatives of a patient in Intensive Care and all of the outdated magazines that littered the coffee-table. She also got to know Jeremy Foster's mother very well after a particularly long angst-filled night when Jeremy had nearly lost his fight for life.

Yet for all that she knew she loved Samuel, the wretched days that ensued as Anna hovered on the side-lines of life served only to ram home how little she knew about him.

'She's improving—that's good.'

Erin turned from the sink, stirring her coffee for some-thing to do as Samuel entered the tiny waiting room. Putting a finger up to her lips, she gestured towards a sleeping Mavis Foster before she wearily sat down. 'You tell me "critical but stable", "hanging in there", it all means nothing to me.' They spoke in low tones so as not to disturb Mavis. 'Until she wakes up and can talk, I won't believe my sister's going to be all right. The charge nurse said they're going to try and extubate her later this morning. Hopefully it will go well.'

Samuel didn't anything. Instead, he came and sat beside her on the small couch. 'I'm sorry I couldn't come sooner, I've had a few dramas of my own.'

Erin nodded dismissively. It was two a.m. after all, and right now she was simply too tired and too wrapped up in Anna to make polite noises for his excuses.

'Is Jordan here?'

Again Erin nodded. 'He's in with Anna now.' Her voice was flat, subdued, and she didn't look up as she continued talking. 'He blames me for all of this.'

She waited for the platitudes, for the 'you're just imagining it', but for once they didn't come.

'Why?'

His question made her start. 'Because we were rowing. We have been all week.' Erin hesitated. She could hardly tell Samuel what the row was about. 'Jordan feels that if I hadn't put her under so much pressure, if I had only…' Erin closed her eyes, fighting the tears that were forming 'If I somehow…'

A warm, dry hand reached out and held hers. 'Maybe he should be blaming me.'

Erin looked up sharply.

'Or even Jeremy,' Samuel continued.

'Jeremy?' Erin said, bewildered 'What on earth has Jeremy got to do with this?'

For a moment he didn't answer but his hand tightened around hers. 'About as much as you have. If Jeremy hadn't been speeding, and wrapped his car around the hospital gates. If I hadn't been so emotional after he came into A and E and turned up on your doorstep. If we hadn't made love… Well, you wouldn't have ended up rowing with Anna and, of course, none of this would have happened.'

An involuntary smile wobbled on the edge of her lips. 'I guess,' she said slowly. 'If you put it like that.'

'Jordan is probably feeling as guilty as hell himself. He was in Sydney when it happened, he knew she was upset, knew she was feeling unwell and from her notes Jordan knew her peak-flow readings had dropped off over the last couple of days. Maybe *he* should have done more, insisted that Anna see her GP or come to A and E.'

'He couldn't have envisaged this,' Erin said defensively 'It's not his fault.'

'Exactly,' Samuel said firmly, his hand tightening around hers. 'It's absolutely no one's fault. It's just the way it is and that, Erin, is that. It would be nice to think we play a part in our own destiny and that of everyone else, but sometimes we don't. Fate, chance—whatever you want to call it—always wins. Every person that comes through the doors of A and E wants to push the rewind button on the last couple of hours or days. To do something, *anything* different that might have changed the outcome. Everyone has their own story.'

Something in his words reached her and Erin's hand gripped his hand tighter. 'I know what you mean. Earlier, I mean before this all happened when we were filming…' He watched as the colour returned to her cheeks and the excitement mounted in her voice. 'I was thinking the same. How it's like a kaleidoscope…' She gave him a shy smile. 'I know you'll think I'm crazy but I want to do nursing.'

She waited for him to laugh but his mirth never came. 'You'd make a wonderful nurse. How long have you been thinking about it?'

'Since… I'm not sure really when it started, but the

time I spent in A and E, well, like I said, my job doesn't have the drama I crave, sick as it may sound. It's not that I enjoy seeing people suffer, it's just watching all you do down there. You really do make a difference.'

'It would be a big task. Giving up all you've got. Going back to being a student. Do you really think you could do it all again?'

'I don't know,' she replied honestly. 'I like to think I'm not materialistic but, as you pointed out, it's easy to say money doesn't matter when you've got it. If I go ahead and buy Anna out, this time around I really will be a poor student. It doesn't sound quite so appealing when you're nearing thirty.'

'So sell.'

His words hit home.

'Surely your parents would have wanted you to follow your dreams? If you sell you'd be able to study full time and still be able to afford a home of your own, though obviously not as big as where you are now. This could be their gift to you. Even in death they're still looking after you. Isn't that what any parent would want, to help their children attain their dreams? Anna and Jordan could have their nice little picket-fence home and you could follow your heart. You really would be a fabulous nurse.'

Erin took a sip of her coffee and grimaced. 'It's gone cold.' Replacing the cup on the table, she continued in a strained voice. 'I'm not stalking you or anything crazy like that. I'm not considering a career change just so I can see more of you. You mustn't think that.'

'My ego's not that big.' He gave a hollow laugh. 'Why would you say such a thing?'

Erin heard the genuine bewilderment in his voice and looked up. For the first time she looked at him properly. He was wearing jeans and a T-shirt yet despite the casual attire he looked anything but relaxed. She took in the heavy circles under his eyes and the unkempt hair.

'Because our one night together meant everything to me and nothing to you. Who could blame me for wanting to prolong it?'

His hand, which had held hers so tightly, released its grip. She saw a flash of pain darken his features. 'Erin, don't.'

'Why, Samuel? I'm sorry I'm not some sophisticated lover who can say no strings. You hurt me, and you cheapened me…'

He was on his feet in an instant, marching over to the tiny window and staring unseeingly at the night sky outside. She could see the tension in his shoulders as he struggled to respond.

'Erin, I never ever meant to hurt you. Don't say I cheapened you. It wasn't like that and we both know it.' He turned and Erin was shocked by the raw emotion she saw in his face. 'You are the most beautiful, warm, loving woman I have ever met. There has never been or ever will be a woman I want more than you. Please, believe that. Never feel cheap because of what we did.' He turned back to the window and Erin watched, bemused, as he forced himself to continue. 'I'm doing you a favour. I can't expect you to understand but I'm asking you to believe me. I'm no good for you.'

'How can you say that? How can you know what's good for me?' she pleaded. But her words fell on deaf ears.

'You have to move on, Erin, forget what happened. It can never happen again.' He was fighting to keep his voice down. 'We're not going to end up together, Erin, it's just not going to happen. I'm asking you to let it go. Please?'

How could she respond to that? He had left no room for Erin to argue. Dejectedly she sat there, staring at her cold coffee, listening to the hateful tick of the clock. 'The show airs tonight,' she said finally. 'The A and E girls are all coming in and cracking open some champagne. If Anna's stable I said I'd go down and watch it with them. Will you come?' Her voice was flat, her words full of the need to say something, anything other than what was on both their minds.

Samuel turned. 'Are you going to show the empty medical and coronary care beds?'

Erin didn't answer.

'I couldn't blame you if you did.'

'How did you hear about that?'

'Not much gets past me.'

Getting up, she tipped her cold drink down the sink. 'No,' she replied finally. 'I managed to talk Mark out of it. So, are you coming down?'

For what seemed an eternity he stared at her. She longed to cross the room, to fall into his arms, but instead she sat there, staring into his smoky eyes.

Samuel finally spoke. 'I'd better be going.' He crossed the room and only when he got to the door did he turn.

'I'm sorry for your pain, Erin, I really am.'

As the morning sun streamed through the flimsy curtains and Erin and Mavis were woken by a cheerful domestic emptying the waiting-room bin and vacuuming the carpet, the charge nurse came in, smiling.

'Good news.'

They both looked up hopefully. A comradeship had developed and though both desperately wanted the good news to be directed at them, they held hands, determined to be pleased for the other if the news wasn't what they were praying for.

'Good news all round, actually.' The charge nurse smiled at them both. 'Your son has stabilised. He's fighting the ET tube, Mrs Foster, and the anaesthetist is going to extubate him. I know it's the third go but he really is looking a lot better this morning.' She turned to Erin. 'The anaesthetist has already extubated Anna.' She put up her hands as Erin went to speak. 'Now, she's still very drowsy and we're still watching her closely, but she's turned a huge corner. Jordan's with her at the moment and we're just going to give her a wash and then you can come in and see her. Mrs Foster, as soon as I can, I'll be back out.'

The two women hugged each other as the charge nurse bustled away.

'I told you things always seem better in the morning,' Mavis said through her tears.

Erin hugged her tightly. 'You did, too. When you go and see Jeremy, Mavis, remember to tell him he's going to be a star.'

Mavis wiped her cheeks with a lacy handkerchief. 'I'd better ring around and make sure everyone tapes it. He'd never forgive me if I didn't get a copy.'

Erin laughed. 'I'm sure the network will be able to stretch to a freebie.'

'When he gets better I'm going to give him a piece of my mind,' Mavis said in a quavering voice. 'He's in his mid-thirties after all. It's time he settled down and found a nice girl and gave me some grandchildren to fuss over and worry about, instead of him.'

'You tell him,' Erin said, smiling. 'And if he doesn't listen, give me five minutes with him. Jeremy Foster is responsible for my first grey hair and that's no lie.'

Though both woman joked and smiled, each knew that they had been blessed and that they were the lucky ones—the ones who got to see their relatives leave the intensive care unit and move onto the wards. For too many others the story ended right there in that bland room.

Though improving rapidly, Anna was still very unwell and Erin couldn't keep the surprise from her voice when the charge nurse informed her that they were moving Anna onto the main ward that very afternoon.

'So soon? But she still seems to be needing nebulisers all the time, and she seems so ill.'

The charge nurse nodded. 'It maybe is a bit quicker than we'd like but unfortunately we need the bed for a ventilated patient. Anna will be moved to a high-dependency bed. She'll still be watched very closely.'

And with that Erin had to be satisfied. Still, it didn't stop her worrying and she hovered closely all day. Anna was moved to a six-bedded ward. She was by far the youngest and most of the other patients lay quietly as Anna's gurney was wheeled onto the ward, seemingly oblivious of the new arrival. All except one lady who, despite her jerking, thrashing movements on the bed, looked on. Erin smiled somewhat self-consciously and the woman continued to thrash around the bed, her mouth contorting as if she was trying to speak.

The nurses pulled the curtains around Anna as they transferred her onto the bed. Jordan was outside, making a telephone call, so Erin stood alone and uncomfortable, weighed down by the amazing amount of property Anna seemed to have collected over the last few days.

An ear-piercing shriek made Erin turn suddenly.

'Be with you in a moment, Patty,' one of the nurses called from behind the curtain.

Patty didn't seem to be in pain, but the jerking movements and shrieking continued and she was looking directly at Erin. Blushing self-consciously, Erin made her way over.

'Hi, Patty, I'm Erin. They're just putting my sister Anna into bed.' How much Patty understood Erin wasn't sure, but she watched with satisfaction as her words seemed to placate the woman and the shrieking stopped. Yet still the awkward relentless motions continued.

Gradually, with the help of Jordan, Erin had pieced together what had happened. Samuel had been right. Anna's peak-flow readings had indeed been dropping off—an ominous sign for asthmatics that they needed to be reviewed. Anna had finally realised she needed to be seen and at Jordan's insistence had agreed to go to the doctor that morning. After he'd left for the airport Anna had tried to get an appointment but none had been available until the afternoon. She'd decided to go into work where she'd gradually worsened. Too sick to drive, Anna had taken a taxi home. The rest was guesswork. Had she gone home to get another pump? Why hadn't she gone straight onto the nebuliser? Why hadn't she rung the doctors and insisted they see her, or called for an ambulance?

There was still a load of questions buzzing in their minds but they both knew Anna wasn't yet up to an inquisition. Erin's and Anna's row was long since forgotten and even Jordan, now that Anna wasn't quite so seriously ill, seemed to have lightened up. He even managed a small apology.

'I was wrong to blame you,' Jordan said as they sat by the bedside, with Anna dozing peacefully. She still had a seemingly inordinate number of drips and tubes, and a huge oxygen mask covered her face, but she actually looked a lot more relaxed out of the intensive care unit.

'I've been blaming everyone except myself, actually,' Jordan continued. 'I should have realised how bad she was, taken her to the doctor myself.'

Samuel had been right yet again. 'It was no one's fault. Let's all just be grateful things worked out.'

'Time for physio.' Heather, the physiotherapist, appeared brightly by the bed.

'It seems a shame to wake her, she must be exhausted,' Erin said, looking over at the bed.

'She needs her physio,' Heather said firmly. 'We shouldn't be too long.'

Jordan yawned. 'I might go and grab a coffee from the canteen. Are you coming?'

Erin shook her head. 'I've had enough coffee to last a lifetime. I'll just wait in the day room.'

As Jordan wandered off, Erin made her way out of the ward, stopping to chat with one of the nurses who had called her over as she hurriedly tried to feed Patty.

'Fay from A and E rang earlier. She said you're to be sure and go down there tonight.' All the staff knew about the show and everywhere Erin went she was questioned about it.

Erin laughed. 'It depends how brave I'm feeling. The A and E girls are hardly the sort you want to get on the wrong side of. I might be better watching it at home alone.'

A patient's buzzer interrupted their light-hearted chatter and Erin watched as the nurse looked around for a colleague.

'I'm sure it will be fine…'

Again the buzzer sounded impatiently. The nurse turned and apologetically smiled at Patty. 'Sorry, Patty, most of the staff are at lunch and the other nurses must be caught up. Do you mind if I get that buzzer?'

Patty let out a wail of frustration as the nurse put the carton down on the bedside table.

'I don't mind feeding Patty until you come back,' Erin ventured as the buzzer sounded yet again.

Jane hesitated for a moment. 'Well, if you're sure. Patty can't have any thin fluids—she has trouble swallowing. Just feed her this slowly. I shan't be long.'

Gratefully she rushed off and Erin nervously picked up the bowl.

'Go easy on me, Patty,' Erin pleaded as she loaded the spoon. 'I'm new to all this.'

Slowly, messily they got through the meal, and by the time the plate had been scraped clean a firm friendship had been forged. Patty, Erin noticed, seemed to visibly relax if Erin carried on talking, as if somehow the diversion of conversation made the thrashing movements ease. For Erin this was no great hardship as she loved to chat about anything and anyone, even sloppy mashed potato.

'Just what do you think you're doing?'

Erin dropped the spoon and almost the plate as Samuel's angry voice interrupted her chatter.

'The nurse was busy and Patty was hungry. I did ask first. I didn't just go ahead and feed her without checking it was all right. What was I supposed to do, leave her sitting there, hungry?' She stared at him defiantly before adding cheekily, 'Anyway, we're not in your beloved department now, you can't bawl me out here.'

She had meant it as a joke, an attempt to lighten the mood. Never in a million years could she have envisaged what was about to come.

'We may not be in my department but as it happens to be my mother you're feeding, I have every right to question what you are doing.' Brushing past her, he made his way to the bedside where he kissed Patty on the cheek and pulled up a chair.

'Patty's your mother...' Erin was for once completely lost for words. 'I'm sorry, I just didn't realise...' she faltered. But Samuel brushed away her apologies. Opening the top drawer of the locker, he retrieved the day's newspaper and, after rummaging in his pocket, threw in a dollar. 'The nurses catch the paper boy for me when he comes round,' he said by way of an explanation as Erin carried on staring.

'I'm sorry for shouting. It was nice of you to feed her—she enjoys her meals. Oh, by the way, Erin, her name's Patricia, not Patty. I've already told the nurses to stop calling her that. She hates having her name shortened.' Samuel turned to the sports page quickly but not before Erin caught the flash of pain on his face. 'Or at least she used to hate it,' he said sadly and almost to himself. 'At least she used to.'

The afternoon dragged on for ever. Achingly aware of Samuel sitting on the opposite side of the room, Erin was completely unable to relax. All the magazines she had with her she'd read at least five times and Anna slept on soundly. Samuel, of course, seemed completely unaffected by Erin's presence. He calmly read the paper from back to front, now and then stopping to read to Patricia a particularly amusing line or to tell her about certain events, but on the whole he sat in silence. Patricia in turn seemed a lot happier when her son was around, even to the extent that by late afternoon she had dozed off. Erin couldn't help but notice over the top of her magazine that in sleep the spasmodic, relentless movements halted and Patricia looked like any other woman taking an afternoon nap.

Samuel caught her staring and Erin blushed as she diverted her eyes back to her magazine and pretended to read. Her heart rate picked up as a shadow fell over her page. Looking up, she saw Samuel standing over her.

'Mum's asleep. I'm going to get some air. Will you join me?'

Of course, Erin didn't need to ask Jordan's permission but she turned to him all the same. 'I shan't be long.'

Jordan gave her a tiny wink and a friendly smile. 'Take all the time you need. We shan't be going anywhere.'

'In that case, we might grab some supper,' Samuel said, to Erin's complete surprise and utter delight. 'Do you want us to bring you anything back?'

A few days spent surviving on Cellophane-wrapped sandwiches made even the most polite of people rewrite their standards. 'Normally I'd say, no, I'm fine, but the truth is I'm starving. You choose, though, Samuel. Tofu casserole does nothing for me.'

Samuel laughed. 'We'll see what we can do.'

'Jordan seems a lot friendlier,' Samuel observed as they came out into the low evening sun.

Erin fished in her bag for her sun glasses. 'He's actually been really good. I think I misjudged him—he's not that bad really.'

'Amazing what a near-death experience will do to even the blandest personality,' Samuel said dryly, and they both laughed. They walked in silence for a while, Samuel taking her elbow occasionally and directing her down certain side streets. He obviously knew where he was going. Erin didn't care where he was taking her. Just being in his presence was enough for her and she walked quickly beside him, slightly breathless form the exertion of keeping up with his long, effortless strides.

'Here we are.'

They had turned onto the Beach Road. Patrons from the pubs and cafés sat on the pavement tables outside, enjoying the warm evening, but Samuel turned and made his way inside a smart-looking bistro and purposefully headed up the stairs.

'Good evening, Mr Donovan.' The waitress smiled at Samuel and cast an inquisitive look in Erin's direction. 'The usual table?'

She led them over to the balcony where they sat opposite each other as the waitress handed them the menus.

'Can I get you both a drink?'

'A beer would be great.' He looked questioningly at Erin. 'I'm sorry. What would you like?'

'A gin and tonic would be lovely.' Erin studied the menu closely, trying to quell the butterflies that were leaping in her stomach. It was all simply too good to be true. This morning, as she and Mavis had been praying for their loved ones to simply make it through, she could never have envisaged that the day would end as perfectly as this.

Samuel chose the seafood platter and Erin settled for gnocchi with a creamy pumpkin sauce.

'We've a friend back at the hospital to feed as well,' Samuel said to the waitress, 'so could I order the spicy chicken and rice to be ready when we go?'

'Sure,' the waitress replied easily. 'No worries.'

The bay glittered before them, the evening sky was aglow with burnt oranges and reds and boats were making their way back. The water looked so close that Erin felt she could hold out her hand over the edge of the balcony and touch it. She could hear the hum of jet skis in the distance. It was the perfect romantic setting with the perfect man, but Erin knew by the wary look on his face that romance wasn't on Samuel's mind.

'You must come here a lot,' Erin said, 'to have tabs on the best table.'

He took a long drink of his beer. 'Quite often, but normally I'm on the orange juice. I like to come here if I'm on all weekend—it's good to get out for a couple of hours.'

'You're not on call tonight, then?' Erin asked, gesturing to the beer.

'I've got a couple of weeks off.'

'Holidays, that's nice. You need a break, especially with your mum being unwell.'

Samuel took another drink of his beer before he spoke. 'I'm on compassionate leave, Erin,' he said slowly, and she looked up, horrified. 'Mum came into hospital a few days ago because she's taken a turn for the worse. She's dying, Erin.'

Erin's search for the right words to say was mercifully put on hold for a moment as the waitress returned with herb bread and a huge bowl of salad. But as she left, Erin did the only thing that felt instinctively right and reached over the small table and grabbed his hand. 'I'm so sorry, Samuel, I really am.'

She loosed his hand when the waitress brought their food, and for a while they ate in silence.

Once they'd finished their meal, Samuel continued, 'My mother has Huntington's chorea—have you heard of it?'

Erin thought for a moment, her brow furrowing as she tried to remember. 'No, I don't think so.'

'I wanted to tell you, you have to believe that, Erin, and then again I didn't—it's not an easy thing to tell anyone. One never can work out the right time to slip that little gem into a conversation.' He gave a hollow laugh and Erin realised with a sinking feeling that the bad news had only just started.

'Huntington's disease is a progressive neurological disorder. Of course, every case is different but symptoms generally appear in the thirty to forty age group.' At first Samuel had sounded completely like the doctor he was, talking about a disease and its progression in authoritative but unemotional tones. It was only when he completed his speech that Erin heard the raw anguish in his voice. 'Death from the disease is inevitable—it's the period before that which is hell.' He swallowed a mouthful of beer before he continued. 'I watched my mother go from a vivacious, eloquent woman to what she is today. I watched my father, exhausted from looking after her, literally die from a broken heart. And the best bit of it all was that, being a doctor, from the day of her diagnosis I knew what could be in store for me.'

Erin looked at him, nonplussed.

'It's hereditary, Erin.' The words were the words of the executioner. Erin felt a spasm of pain grip her heart as she thought of this hideous disease invading Samuel. The thought of that beautiful, intelligent mind slowly being eradicated... She wanted to shout out, to declare to the world the unfairness of what she was hearing, but instead she took a huge slug of her gin, knowing instinctively that she had to let him speak first, to let him tell her how it was, how it had been for him. Only then could she truly try to understand.

'I was newly married at the time we found out. Frances was a doctor as well, so she knew the score completely. At first she was supportive, or tried to be, but you can't hide the smell of fear. She wanted me to take the test.'

'There's a test you can have?' Erin asked, for the first

time a ray of hope appearing. 'You mean you don't automatically inherit it?'

Samuel nodded. 'It's a fifty-fifty chance, straight down the line. Either you carry the gene or you don't. If you don't carry it, you're fine. You can go on with your life, have children with no fear of passing it on. But if you've inherited it, there's no hope. Unless you're run over by a bus or something else gets you, Huntington's will definitely get you in the end.' Erin tried to take it all in as she sat there quietly, listening.

'I decided not to take the test.'

Erin didn't say anything. There wasn't much she could say after all, so instead she took another sip of her drink and let him continue. 'Frances agreed with me at first. The best thing was to concentrate on helping Mum and Dad and try to carry on as normal. The only thing I was adamant about was that there would be no children. I could live with taking my chances but it simply wasn't fair to inflict these odds on my own child. So I had a vasectomy. I had a lot of counselling beforehand at my doctor's insistence, but I knew that at that time I was doing the right thing. Anyway, Frances and I limped along but it was just a façade.'

'She left you?' Erin asked incredulously.

'She couldn't handle it. I don't blame her for a second. Huntington's stretches the marriage vows of ''in sickness and in health''. After Dad died, I realised I was ready to find out. Everyone's different, but for me the time had come and I was ready to know. I took the test last year.'

Erin's eyes were brimming with tears at the thought of the hell he had been through but mainly the terror of what he would say next.

'It was negative.'

Her heart soared. 'You mean, you don't have it? Oh, Samuel, that's wonderful.'

But he sat quite still, staring at his glass for the longest time until he finally dragged his eyes up to hers. 'I had a vasectomy, Erin. Even with the best surgeon reversing it, there's no guarantee I can have children. Do you understand now why it would be unfair of me to pursue a relationship with you?'

But Erin was walking on air. She had seen the jaws of death clamping around her beloved Samuel and he had been snatched away. Nothing could sour this sweet moment. 'We can work things out,' she said, half laughing and half crying with the emotion of the moment. 'It's you I want, Samuel, and it always has been from the moment I met you. Children aren't everything.'

But he steadfastly refused to be comforted by her words. 'Maybe not now, Erin, but I saw the way you looked when Deborah Grayson had her baby. How can I marry you, knowing I may not be able to give you babies? How can I take the joy of motherhood away from you?'

'We could adopt or try IVF. There's millions of possibilities if that's the path we decide to take. But it doesn't matter at the moment,' she said.

'It's easy to sit here and say it doesn't matter now, but I've already had one marriage die because of this illness. I can't watch another one fade away.'

'No.' Erin's voice came out more loudly than she'd intended and several other diners looked around at them. 'No,' she said more quietly, but the urgency was still in her voice. 'Your first marriage died because your wife didn't love you enough. Because she wasn't prepared to stand by you through the bad times. The disease was just an excuse. It would have ended sooner or later anyway.'

'You can't say that for sure,' he said wearily. 'Don't judge Frances so harshly Erin, this really is a terrible disease. Are you really trying to tell me that had I told you then that the test was positive, you'd still be sitting here?'

'Absolutely,' Erin said resolutely, but Samuel shook his head disbelievingly.

'Maybe for the remainder of the meal, Erin, maybe for a week or two afterwards. But at some point you'd head down to the library or look up the disease on the computer and realise what you were getting into.'

'And you think that once I found out I'd leave you?'

Samuel nodded. 'It's irrelevant anyway. As I said, I don't have the disease.'

'Oh, no, Samuel.' Her voice was trembling with emotion. 'I'd say that it's extremely relevant.' He looked up sharply as her tone cut through him, surprise visible on his face as he watched the anger mounting in her eyes. 'Would you leave me? I mean, if the roles were reversed.'

'Of course not,' he said immediately and with conviction. 'Of course I wouldn't.'

'So why do you think that I would?'

For a moment he didn't answer. His eyes turned to the fading sunset and he drank in the view for a moment before he finally responded. 'Because you deserve better.' His voice hardened. 'As I said before, I'm not the marrying kind.'

'And you're not going to change your mind? After all that's been said, with all that we feel, you're still sticking by that?'

The pain that seared through Erin was indescribable as slowly but surely he nodded his head.

'Maybe you're right. Maybe I do deserve better.' She

watched as the glass he had been lifting to his mouth paused midway. 'Like a man that trusts and loves me enough to know I'd always be there for him. I had this vision that when I fell I love, when Mr Right finally came along—and, believe me, it's been quite a wait.' She added, 'I had the craziest notion that my feelings would be reciprocated, that he'd love me as completely and utterly as I loved him, that we'd face obstacles and life's problems together. Believe it or not, Samuel, everyone has their share of problems. Everyone, not just you. Now, if you have so little faith in my love, in my ability to care and be with you through it all, then there's really no point in continuing this conversation…'

The waitress returned with the bill and a container. 'Here's your chicken. Can I get you guys another drink?'

Erin took the container and stood up. 'Not for me, thanks, but Mr Donovan would love another beer.'

As the waitress walked off Samuel stood up. 'Sit down, Erin, have another drink. We need to talk.'

But Erin's mind was made up. 'No, Samuel, we've done enough talking. I'm going back to the hospital.' She looked at her watch. 'My show starts in an hour, I promised the guys and girls in A and E I'd watch it with them.' Erin picked up the bill and then replaced it firmly on the table, leaning over and lowering her voice so he had to strain to catch what she was saying. 'As you seem to think I'm just an airhead out for your body and money, Samuel, I'm going to act like one. You can pay for dinner.'

'What on earth are you talking about?' he asked, bewildered by her statement.

'Well, as you so obviously don't believe in love, why else would I be here?'

She held it together all the way down the bistro's steps

all the way out onto the Beach Road. Only when she was safely in the darkness of a side street did Erin let the tears come. And she cried like she had never cried before in her life, half running, oblivious of the curious looks of passers-by as great sobs convulsed her body. It was all so unfair. That rotten, insidious disease had shattered so many lives, and now it was ruining hers, for she knew that Samuel Donovan was the only man she would ever love.

Jordan was too polite to comment on her swollen eyes and reddened cheeks.

Erin handed him his dinner. 'I'll be down in A and E for the next couple of hours if you need me, Jordan, and then I think I'll head off home. Are you going to stay here tonight?'

Jordan shrugged as he dived into his chicken. 'I'm still working on it. The charge nurse apparently isn't too keen on relatives staying over, but she did say she'd think about it. Given that Anna has only just come out of Intensive Care. Even if I just crash in the day room for the night. I just don't feel right leaving her yet.'

Erin nodded. 'She's lucky to have you,' she said softly.

Jordan looked up from his dinner. 'Do you really think so, Erin?' And the way he said it sounded for all the world as if Erin's opinion really mattered to him.

'Of course she is. You're lucky to have each other.'

Making her way down the ward, she paused for a second beside Patricia's bed. Now that she knew, she could see the resemblance between her and Samuel. Patricia's hair was grey but it was as thick and straight as Samuel's. They had the same high cheekbones, the same straight nose. How hard it must have been for Patricia. Those years of uncertainty, knowing she could have passed this disease on to her own son. Had she been well enough to understand the good news when Samuel finally took the test? Erin felt the hot sting of tears prick her eyes. 'Don't worry, Patricia,' she whispered. 'I'll look after him.' And taking a seat by Patricia's bedside, she added in a subdued tone, 'If he lets me.'

'He told you?' Fay had none of Jordan's reserve. One look at her swollen lids and she had dragged Erin into an empty cubicle, pulling the curtain behind her.

'Yes, he told me,' Erin responded tearfully, sitting down on the gurney and hardly noticing as it lurched forward. 'How long have you known?'

Putting on the brake first, Fay climbed up beside Erin. 'Years, since his mum was diagnosed. It was just so awful for everyone. His mother was such a beautiful woman. All she was worried about was Samuel. "At least he's married," she said. "At least he's got Frances."' Erin heard the sarcasm in her voice. 'Fat lot of good Frances turned out to be.'

'But it must have been hard for her,' Erin said quickly, though why she was defending Frances she wasn't sure. 'Samuel said—'

'Samuel makes excuses for her. Sure, it must have been awful for her, for all of them, but she never even gave them a chance to work things through. Within three months of his mother's diagnosis she was out of there. She blamed it on the fact they couldn't have children but it was just an excuse. She was terrified of ending up playing nursemaid.' Fay suddenly stood up.

'He did tell you about the vasectomy, didn't he? I'm not breaking any confidences?'

Erin nodded resignedly. 'He told me.'

'I'm sorry for trying to matchmake, Erin. It was just so obvious to me that you were meant for each other. I don't know, I just assumed you'd be able to cope with the news. I shouldn't have interfered.'

Erin looked up, confused. 'What are you saying?'

Fay looked embarrassed. 'Well, you're obviously upset. I guess the fact Samuel mightn't be able to have children must have put you off—'

She never got to finish her sentence. Erin leapt to her feet. Standing angrily, she literally shook with emotion as she spoke. 'Fay, the furthest thing from my mind when Samuel told me was whether or not we could have children together. I was just relieved to find out that there was a reason for all this pain. And as I heard the story, all I could feel was utter joy that he was going to be all right. It's Samuel who can't deal with not having children. It's Samuel who thinks I'm the sort of person that would walk out on him if he'd had the disease. I know he's had a rough time, I know he's been hurt, but if he thinks I'm starting a relationship under the shadow of another woman's mistakes then he's wrong. I want a clean slate. I want a man that can love and trust *me*.'

Fay listened, unblinking, to Erin's speech. 'Your show will be starting soon,' was all she said when Erin had finished. 'You'd better go to the staffroom. The team have put on a bit of a feed—you're the guest of honour.'

Erin gave her a quizzical look. She had expected some response, some comment on her outburst, but Fay had obviously decided she'd heard enough. 'Are you coming?'

Fay nodded. 'I'll be along soon. I've got a few things I need to sort out first. You go ahead.'

CHAPTER ELEVEN

THERE was practically a party going on in the staffroom. The tables were covered with hospital sheets and *everyone*, it seemed, had turned out for the show and brought in some food—chips, popcorn, quiches, cakes, bottles of fizzy drink, even some wine and beers for the staff who weren't on duty. Erin accepted a plastic cup filled to the brim with cheap wine. 'Looks like I'll be getting a taxi home tonight,' she said with a smile. And despite the pain of the previous hours, despite the terror of the last few days, to her utter surprise Erin realised she was actually enjoying herself—at least, as much as one could with a broken heart. Here with this eccentric, vivacious team who cared not only for their patients but also for each other. Who could be bitchy and cliquish one moment and as compassionate and all-encompassing the next. She knew her decision to enter nursing was the right one, and though it was still incredibly early days Erin also knew without a shadow of a doubt that A and E was where she wanted to specialise.

'You realise you're taking your life in your own hands, watching it with us, don't you?' Vicki said teasingly. 'If it's not flattering we might end up wheeling you down to the plaster room for a fitting.'

'A fitting?' Erin questioned.

'For a full body plaster. And if the show's really bad, we mightn't be able to find the plaster saw for a few hours.'

Everyone laughed, Erin included, but for the hundredth

time since Anna's illness she breathed a huge sigh of relief that she'd stood her ground with Mark and refused to show the empty hospital beds.

Though she had seen all the footage and the final version several times, although she knew there were going to be no surprises, Erin felt a surge of excitement as someone dimmed the lights and the familiar signature tune started. Frantically she glanced around the darkened room for Samuel and Fay but they were nowhere to be seen. Erin felt a surge of disappointment. Fay must have been caught up, and Samuel... She swallowed hard as she fought the image of him sitting alone on the balcony in the darkness staring into his beer, thinking about his mother, his father, Frances and, Erin admitted, herself. For a second she was tempted to forget the show and run back to the bar, to comfort him, to somehow reach him, but deep inside she knew that wasn't the answer. He had to be the one to come to her.

There were a few catcalls as the presenter mentioned Erin's name and the hospital and suddenly there she was, immaculate in her cream suit, walking along the hospital's main entrance towards the camera, inviting the viewers to join her for the next twenty-four hours in the accident and emergency department of Melbourne City. A manicured hand that most definitely *wasn't* hers was shown in close-up, pushing open the black swing doors as the department came into view.

Erin heard the staffroom door open. Turning slightly, her heart skipped a few beats as Samuel and Fay entered. Fay noisily made her way over to a sofa and grabbed a bowl of chips on the way, while Samuel stood quietly at the back of the room, his wide shoulders resting slightly against the wall, his haughty profile achingly familiar in the soft darkness. She longed for him to come over, for everyone to move up one as he came and sat beside her, but instead he simply stayed there, watching intently, his eyes never once turning towards Erin.

And for the next hour they all sat transfixed, watching, fascinated, as Erin took the viewers on the most amazing journey. From the most banal of injuries to the most critically wounded, all were shown tastefully. And the staff's ability to cope, the chameleon-like way they behaved, the tears, the humour—it was all there and all explained.

There was Elsie, proud and dignified, chastising the nursing staff for fussing, and there she was again, desperately ill, her tiny face lost under the oxygen mask as the staff worked intently on her. The frustrated patient losing his temper at being forced to wait cut briefly back to the resuscitation room and Elsie, and somehow it magnified the fact that no one really knew what went on behind closed doors. There were scenes of drunks waiting noisily in the waiting room alongside the sophisticated friends of the Graysons, interspersed with the contorted face of Deborah Grayson in labour, pushing her daughter into the world.

It was truly inspirational, and all watched, riveted. The only sounds were the occasional laugh or groan, but when Mr Reed appeared on screen the whole room fell silent. They watched together as Jeremy, haughty yet endearingly nervous, explained to Mr Reed the magnitude of the situation he faced. The clean-up of the resuscitation room was shown—the instruments being replaced, the trolleys being restocked.

And later again Jeremy appeared, exhausted but jubilant, to tell Mrs Reed her husband had made it. Amazingly, Phil had got some footage of Erin talking to Jeremy and, though what had been said hadn't been captured, there was some poignant footage of Jeremy waving goodbye and walking through the black swing doors. A shot of the clock showed it was seven p.m. and Erin's face appeared again. Gone were the theatre greens and she was back in her cream suit.

'And that was the twenty-four hours I spent in the accident and emergency department. But if you've seen the news or read a paper this week, you'll know that it didn't end there. Only minutes after the cameras stopped rolling, the doctor we had just witnessed saving a patient's life was himself involved in a terrible accident. The hospital supplies we saw so recently being replenished were now being used to save him. The staff who had previously been working alongside Mr Foster had to suddenly deal with working not with him but *on* him.

'It was the most sobering moment I have ever faced in my career and one that will stay with me always. We all watch the news and read the papers, we all moan about hospital waiting times and staff shortages. But I hope that by watching this programme you will see, as I did at first hand, the amazing work that goes on in the accident and emergency departments around the country. Next time you hear the sound of a siren cutting through a lazy afternoon, be reminded of the precariousness of life. And also draw some comfort from the fact that in a resuscitation room somewhere there's a group of talented, dedicated people checking their equipment and pulling on their latex gloves, getting ready to do battle to save a fellow human being's life.'

The manicured hand was back briefly as the swing doors closed and suddenly the credits were rolling and Erin's name was there. The staff were all cheering and clapping as the lights flicked on.

'Erin, that was amazing,' Vicki yelled above the noise. 'I never realised what a great job we did.'

'I'm going on a diet,' Louise said, cutting herself an extremely generous piece of mud cake. 'On Monday,' she added.

The chattering died down as Samuel moved forward. Everyone looked up at him as he started to speak.

'It's no secret that I had my reservations about the cameras coming into the department,' he said to the hushed room. 'And as wonderful as tonight's show was, if the board asked me to do the same thing next week I would still have the same reservations. The reason for the success of tonight is due entirely to Erin. I know personally that tonight's show could have painted an entirely different picture of our department. The fact that we're all smiling and cheering is because of the integrity of Erin Casey. I think we should all raise our glasses, or rather our plastic cups, to her.'

Erin blushed furiously as she accepted the praise and then it was her turn to speak. Ever emotional, her eyes brimmed with tears as she looked around the room.

'It's actually me who should be thanking you, and I think we all know that. I only hope that the department can benefit in some small way from this exercise. Thanks, everyone.' She raised her cup to the staff, to her friends, and hastily wiped away a tear which had escaped.

Jenny's head popped around the door. 'We need the trauma team. MVA coming in.'

And that was that. The staff started to disperse. The night team made their way out to face whatever it was that was coming in and the day staff began to collect their bags. Erin looked around hopefully but Samuel was nowhere to be seen. He must have gone to help with the MVA or gone back up to sit with his mother. A couple of staff listlessly started to clear away the mess till Fay shooed them out. 'I'm sure this lot will be polished off by the night staff.' Once alone, Fay turned to her. 'You did a great job. You must be feeling pretty proud.'

Erin shrugged modestly.

'It's going to do your career a lot of good,' Fay said brightly, but Erin shook her head.

'It might if I were staying, but I've decided to study nursing.' She searched Fay's face for her reaction and was relieved to see her smiling.

'You'll be wonderful. If you need any help with the application forms, you let me know.'

'Thanks.'

There was long silence before Fay continued, 'I misjudged you—I'm sorry.'

'What are you talking about?'

'I should have know you would never be so superficial as to run a mile because of Samuel's...well, you know,' she said uncomfortably.

'It doesn't make any difference anyway,' Erin said sadly. 'He's obviously made up his mind he doesn't want me.'

'Then he's mad.' Fay sad fiercely. 'And if it's any consolation, you know how I told you I'd only lost my temper twice in this department before and each time it was totally merited?'

Erin nodded.

'Well, as from an hour ago you can make it three times, and I don't regret a moment of it.'

Erin managed a wobbly smile. 'Thanks, Fay,' she said, her voice choked with the emotion of the night. 'I mean that. Thank you for everything.'

She made her way through the department. Pushing open the black swing doors, she caught sight of her hand—scrawny and pale, with bitten nails. It just about summed up her mood really—so much for the polished façade that had appeared onscreen. Maybe she should book in for a manicure?

'Erin?'

The sound of Samuel's voice caught her off guard and she swung around. As he walked out of the shadows of the darkened corridor she thought her heart would burst with the strain of not running to him.

'I wanted to speak to you after the show but the ward paged me. Mum's slipped into unconsciousness.'

His face was etched with pain and she longed with all her heart to comfort him, but it simply wasn't her place. Samuel had made that perfectly clear.

'I seem to have spent the entire evening being told what a fool I am. I never realised our relationship was such public knowledge.'

Erin scuffed the floor with her foot. 'I might have said something to Fay.'

'Oh, it wasn't just Fay, though she certainly gave me a hard time.'

Erin looked up in astonishment 'Who else, then?'

'Jordan, and then your sister.'

'Jordan? But I didn't think he approved of us. And as for Anna, she's been asleep.'

Samuel managed a wry chuckle. 'She woke up for five minutes and, believe me, she let me have it. And I thought she was the reserved one.'

'I'm sorry,' Erin said awkwardly. 'She doesn't know all the circumstances.'

'Neither does Mavis Foster, but that hasn't stopped her from putting her ten cents' worth in.'

'Mavis Foster?' Erin said incredulously. 'But how on earth did she know anything?'

'I think Mavis must have been pretending to be asleep when we had our talk in the ICU waiting room. One thing you ought to know about hospitals, Erin, before you apply to do your nursing, is that where there's smoke there's fire. If there's even a hint of a good story, in the absence of facts fiction will do very nicely. Our "romance" is even hotter news than your show tonight.'

'I'm sorry if I've caused you any embarrassment,' Erin said quietly. 'It will all blow over in a couple of days. Once Anna's home and I'm out of the hospital, I mean. It will soon be yesterday's news.'

There was a long, long pause. She stared at her hands, at her shoes, at the floor—anywhere rather than at him.

'I don't want it to be yesterday's news.'

Terrified she might be hearing things, Erin carried on staring at her feet. The nail polish on her big toe was looking decidedly worn. Perhaps she should book in for a pedicure as well.

'I want us to be today's news and tomorrow's. I want to give them something to really talk about. I know we hardly know each other and yet I've never known anyone better. I know I've messed things up, I know I've hurt you terribly, but I'm asking you to forgive me, Erin. I love you. I was only trying to protect you.'

She looked up then, her throat tightening as she saw the love burning in his eyes.

'From what?' she gasped.

'From falling in love with me.'

'You could never, ever have stopped that.' She put a tiny unmanicured hand up to his taut, tense cheek. 'I've loved you from the moment I saw you in the admin corridor, and I'll always love you, Samuel.'

He caught her hand and pressed it hard against him, as if drawing from her the strength to go on. 'But what if I can't give you—?'

'Shh, look at me, Samuel.' Shaking, she stroked his

face with her other hand. 'Look at me,' she pleaded, and finally he did. 'What if *I* can't give *you* children? What if we walk out of here now and get run over by an ambulance? And don't say it could never happen—you've seen yourself what a klutz I am.'

The faintest hint of a smile started to appear on his pale lips.

'There's a million what-ifs and only one certainty, Samuel—our love for each other. If we've got that, we can deal with anything, can't we?' She stared into his smoky grey eyes and she felt as if she were staring into the depths of his soul. 'Can't we?' she repeated gently.

He answered her with the sweetest of kisses. Trembling, their lips met in the gentlest of embraces.

'I have to get up to Mum,' he said after an age as he reluctantly pulled away. 'Erin, would you mind coming with me? I don't want to do this on my own.'

'I'd be honoured,' she said, slipping her hand into his.

As they walked hand in hand up the long corridor he stopped for a moment and Erin thought she would weep when she saw the tiniest glimmer of tears in those strong deep eyes. 'I know she probably wouldn't have understood, but I wish I'd managed to tell Mum about us while she was still awake.'

'Oh, I already told her,' Erin said matter-of-factly as she carried on walking. 'Come on, Samuel, we ought to be with her.'

In two giant strides he was alongside her. Reaching for her, he turned her to face him.

'What do you mean, you told her? When?'

'This evening,' Erin said, pulling at his sleeve and hurriedly urging him along. 'My horoscope said that I should say what was on my mind now or I might not get another chance. So I told Patricia not to worry and that I had every intention of marrying you.' She looked up at him out of the corner of her eye as she carried on walking smartly towards the ward.

'Erin Casey, are you proposing to me?'

'Well, yes, I suppose I am,' she said in wonder. 'You don't mind, do you? You're not one of those old-fashioned types who thinks it has to be the man, I hope.'

'And did your horoscope happen to mention anything about a whirlwind romance and a very quick wedding, say, as soon as I can get a licence?'

Erin pondered this for a moment. 'Not in the paper I read today, but I'm sure if I buy every magazine out at the moment I'll be able to find at least one that suggests it.'

At the door of the ward she slipped her hand again into his and he gripped it tightly. It was going to be a long, heart-wrenching night, yet there was no place she would rather be than with this beautiful strong man. Undoubtedly they would have their share of problems in the future, but Erin knew that good times were just around the corner. They would take the rough with the smooth and face the world together.

Some things, Erin mused, were simply meant to be.

EPILOGUE

'SHE'S still very yellow.'

Samuel didn't answer straight away. Instead, he dropped gentle kisses on the tops of his two ladies' heads.

'She's fine,' he said calmly, taking a seat beside the hospital bed as Erin struggled with the feed.

But Erin wasn't about to be placated. 'What if it's something more serious? In one of my nursing books—'

'Erin, she's got a touch of neonatal jaundice. If you don't believe me, surely you can believe the paediatrician. Her blood levels are back and she doesn't even need to go under the phototherapy lights. Now, I hate to pull rank…'

'Again,' Erin groaned.

Samuel grinned. 'From a consultant to a first-year nursing student, a deferred first-year nursing student at that, you have to believe me when I tell you that Grace Patricia Donovan is perfect. You have absolutely nothing to worry about. I dread to think what you'll be like when you do your paeds. I'll have to hide all the books or you'll be diagnosing her with all sorts of ailments.'

'I don't think I'll be going back for a while,' Erin said, gazing fondly at her new baby daughter. 'I know I said I'd only take a term off, but it's a whole new ball game now she's actually here. She really is perfect, isn't she?'

'Perfect,' Samuel agreed. 'I can't wait to have you both home.'

Erin pulled Grace closer. Closing her eyes, she rested against the pillow. Home, she thought fondly. They had been just about to sell, had made all the right noises. Even going as far as having a 'for sale' board erected in the garden. But when push had come to shove, seeing the unnecessary pain it was causing Erin, Samuel had ripped up the estate agent's proposal forms. Now when she closed her eyes and drifted off to her beloved garden, it was dreams of the future and not ghosts from the past that filled Erin's mind. It was Grace running, shrieking with delight, under the sprinklers, joined by the cousin Anna had just told them was on the way and Grace's brothers or sisters yet to come.

'Who's this from?' Samuel asked, breaking into her thoughts as he picked up a huge pink fluffy rabbit from the floor.

'You'll never guess in a million years—Jeremy Foster, of all people. He strolled in about an hour ago, and he looks so well. But most amazing of all, he actually said all the right things—how was *I* feeling, how were *you*, how much did Grace weigh? I had to practically drag out of him how *he* was getting on. He's really changed.' Erin looked up at the sound of Samuel's laughter. 'What's so funny?'

'Actually, I've got a big bit of gossip for you.'

'Tell me,' Erin said impatiently, her eyes widening in anticipation.

'Well, I have it direct from my impeccable source...'

'You mean Fay.'

Samuel nodded as he continued, 'That a certain Jeremy Foster is rather taken with his new intern, and by all accounts there's romance in the air.'

Erin screwed up her nose. 'Hardly a big piece of gossip, Samuel. It sounds more like Jeremy's running true to form. I'm glad he hasn't lost his touch.'

'Well, if you're not going to let me finish...' Samuel said, picking up the paper.

'Tell me!' Erin wailed.

With a lazy grin Samuel slowly replaced the paper until Erin was practically jumping out of the bed in frustration. 'Well, the difference this time is that Jeremy's latest intern is—'

'A man?'

Samuel roared with laughter. 'Erin, you're not going there again, are you? I seem to remember you accused me of being gay once. No, it's better than that. She's about six or seven months pregnant.'

'You're not serious?'

'Deadly. I must admit, Jeremy was the last person I ever thought I'd be discussing the merits of cloth versus disposable nappies with, but, then, stranger things have happened.'

At that moment baby Grace, furious from the lack of attention, let out an angry wail and all thoughts of Jeremy and the world flew from Erin's mind as she concentrated on attaching Grace to her breast.

Samuel leant back in his chair, a huge lump forming in his throat as he gazed with love and pride at his beautiful wife and daughter.

'Stranger things have happened,' he said quietly.

Modern Romance™
...seduction and
passion guaranteed

Tender Romance™
...love affairs that
last a lifetime

Sensual Romance™
...sassy, sexy and
seductive

Blaze
...sultry days and
steamy nights

Medical Romance™
...medical drama on
the pulse

Historical Romance™
...rich, vivid and
passionate

29 new titles every month.

*With all kinds of Romance for
every kind of mood...*

MILLS & BOON®

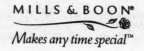

Makes any time special™

MAT4

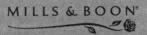

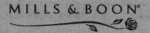

Medical Romance™

BACK IN HER BED *by Carol Wood*

Dr Alison Stewart ended her marriage to Sam when she accused him of having an affair, and he left for Australia. Now her determined husband is back, and the passion between them is still scorching. Sam is back in the marriage bed, but does Alison want him in her life forever?

THE FAMILY HE NEEDS *by Lucy Clark*

Reunited after ten years, it seems that surgeons Zac Carmichael and Julia Bolton are about to rekindle their relationship. But Zac's traumatic past means his instincts are to keep Julia, and her young son Edward, at a distance. Try as he might, however, he knows he can't just walk away from the family he needs…

THE CITY-GIRL DOCTOR *by Joanna Neil*

Suffering from a broken heart, Dr Jassie Radcliffe had left the city to join a challenging rural practice. Her new colleague, Dr Alex Beaufort, made it clear he didn't think she was up to the job, but secretly, he was impressed with Jassie. Then her ex-boyfriend turned up—just as Alex was falling in love with her!

On sale 1st March 2002

Treat yourself this Mother's Day to the ultimate indulgence

3 brand new romance novels and a box of chocolates

= only £7.99

Available from 15th February

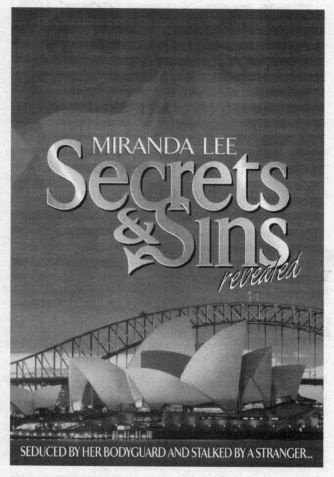

MIRANDA LEE

Secrets & Sins revealed

SEDUCED BY HER BODYGUARD AND STALKED BY A STRANGER...

Available from 15th March 2002

FREE!

2 Books
and a surprise gift!

We would like to take this opportunity to thank you for reading this Mills & Boon® book by offering you the chance to take TWO more specially selected titles from the Medical Romance™ series absolutely FREE! We're also making this offer to introduce you to the benefits of the Reader Service™—

- ★ FREE home delivery
- ★ FREE gifts and competitions
- ★ FREE monthly Newsletter
- ★ Books available before they're in the shops
- ★ Exclusive Reader Service discount

Accepting these FREE books and gift places you under no obligation to buy; you may cancel at any time, even after receiving your free shipment. Simply complete your details below and return the entire page to the address below. *You don't even need a stamp!*

YES! Please send me 2 free Medical Romance books and a surprise gift. I understand that unless you hear from me, I will receive 4 superb new titles every month for just £2.49 each, postage and packing free. I am under no obligation to purchase any books and may cancel my subscription at any time. The free books and gift will be mine to keep in any case.

M2ZEB

Ms/Mrs/Miss/Mr ....Initials.................
BLOCK CAPITALS PLEASE

Surname...

Address...

....

....Postcode ....

Send this whole page to:
UK: The Reader Service, FREEPOST CN81, Croydon, CR9 3WZ
EIRE: The Reader Service, PO Box 4546, Kilcock, County Kildare (stamp required)